Invisible Chapters

Books by Maik Nwosu

Novels
Invisible Chapters
Alpha Song
A Gecko's Farewell
The Book of Everything

Poetry
Suns of Kush
Stanzas from the Underground

Short Stories
Return to Algadez

Drama
A Quintet for Dawn

Invisible Chapters
by
Maik Nwosu

CROSSROADS
New York, 2025

Published by
CROSSROADS
1178 Broadway
3rd Floor, #1333
New York, NY 10001

© 2025 by Maik Nwosu. All rights reserved.
First paperback edition, Tivolick, 1999. Republished by Hybun in 2001 and Beacon in 2015.
Printed in the United States of America

This is a work of fiction. All names, characters, places, and incidents are products of the author's imagination or are used fictitiously.

ISBN 979-8-9904712-2-1

Library of Congress Control Number: 2024905022

For Angela: Maya, always

Book 1
New Maroko

One

Death was on the prowl in New Maroko. It was Christmas season, and the carols filled the air with a winged presence. Haile's Record Shop relentlessly played "White Christmas." *I am dreaming of a White Christmas, just like the ones I used to know.* The phenomenon was new. Usually, Haile, a self-proclaimed Rastafarian, played only the music of the Afrobeat maestro, Fela Anikulapo-Kuti, so much so that his shop had become known as the outer Shrine. The inner Shrine was Fela's nightclub, where Haile was a familiar presence. But this Christmas was special. It marked one year of the interment of Maroko and its resurrection as New Maroko. Like so many others thus uprooted, Haile was celebrating this triumph. He entertained his clients and neighbors with stories of his own experience of "the pure White Christmas."

"The snow falling and carpeting the earth with frozen white streams, the Christmas trees lighting up like beacons, the postman bearing tons of Christmas mail, and everyone remembering everyone else, a time when the great loneliness of the world is transformed into a great communion, a time like no other – the pure White Christmas. Hey, I know what I'm talking about. I've witnessed it once, and that once is forever – forever white."

Haile was a wiry fellow with dreadlocks who had studied African History for four years in the university but eventually failed to earn a degree. In his examination answers, he had insisted on putting historical issues and events in their "proper" perspective – perspectives that many of his teachers had considered outlandish. When he was eventually expelled for repeatedly writing one examination unsuccessfully, he tried to become a singer. But he had his own idea of music, a jarring admixture that producers scoffed at. When he grew tired of "the conspiracy of narrow-minded producers," he set up Haile's Record Shop – in Maroko, which he was wont to describe as "an inner-city Babylon." No one in New Maroko knew he had ever been abroad until that season, and not many people believed him.

In the market streets where sapped men and women dragging malnourished children bent down to strike bargains for *tokunbo* imports – used dresses, shoes, belts, pants, socks, handkerchiefs, and everything else – the bell ringers were loud with their solicitations: "Christmas prices here!" "Buy two for the price of one!" "White Christmas fashion this way, European discounts available!" In the numerous grottos springing up all over, Santa Clauses were becoming cheaper by the day. Many had learned the game of playing Father Christmas – and playing it profitably too. "Chicken Towns," where fowls and foodstuff were on sale at "Christmas prices," suddenly became a pervasive fact of life.

Still, despite the ostensibly triumphal ambience of that Christmas season, the smell of death hung in the air in New Maroko. To many, Haile's "pure White Christmas" was an impossible song.

"White Christmas *ko*, Black Christmas *ni*," Prinzi railed from his café across the road. "'Like the ones I used to know.' The cheek!"

Prinzi, the name he had given himself because he was "a prince of hearts," was a portly, bespectacled fellow who preferred to be known as a writer. He ran a snack bar, "principally for artists," which he preferred to be called a café. "You know, it's so ...literary." His favorite projection was about the great Nigerian novel he would write one day. "You know, it'll start with the beatitude of damnation – 'Blessed are the living for they shall die' – and end with the beatitude of salvation: 'Blessed are the dead for they shall live.' How about that? You know, the best novels are not always those written, even less so those published; the process of writing can constrict or even thwart the greatness of a novel. I know."

Asked why he chose to set up his café in Maroko, Prinzi would chuckle. "My friend, Maroko is the great Nigerian novel writing itself. What more could I possibly ask for? Besides, it's an adjunct of Greater Lagos with some of its advantages but not its steep rent. And there must be something about the slum that draws the artist, something à la mode that makes it almost sacramental to flock to a slum café and profess with passion. Prinzi's Café is a beckoning altar."

Prinzi's claim to being a writer lay in a sole short story he had written, which had been published in a local newspaper. A more or less autobiographical account, he usually referred to the experience narrated – "the latitude to be" – as the key to the Prinzi character. When the story, "Footsteps," was published, Prinzi made several photocopies and mailed them out to a long list of associates, together with elaborate notes. Although he pasted many such copies and notes inside his café, he still did quite some verbal exposition as well.

"More than two decades afterward, the event still grows in me. Life, I learned then and every day since, is freedom. Without that, we might as well have never been born or created. On the other hand, if a man has unlimited freedom, he becomes a winged beast. So, if life is freedom, freedom demands discipline. And what is discipline? One question leads to another – and on and on. That is the vital role of art, you know – to provoke eternal questions."

That season in New Maroko, however, Prinzi was concentrating less on such discourses but directing a string of invectives at Haile's Record Shop. "The fellow has finally lost his little head. How can this 'White Christmas' inanity in an atmosphere of swamping bleakness punctuate his Afrobeat ascensions? If that fellow doesn't stop this nonsense soon, something white is going to happen to him, like a rotten egg in the face or a Plaster of Paris on the neck." But he could not dissuade Haile from playing the song.

"Every day of the year, I play the music of *Baba* himself. Every day. Every year. Everyone knows that. But this year is the Year of Maroko. People who only a year ago were bulldozed to the brink of extinction have today arrived at the brink of salvation. A Christmas of death has been succeeded by that of hope. Why should I not celebrate that?"

"With 'White Christmas'?"

"Well, I know there is such a thing as a pure White

Christmas. I have seen it. But that doesn't really matter. Even if not the lyrics, under the circumstances, the melody of the song is elevating. Should gloom answer gloom? It's the people of the slum who need songs of hope so they can believe again, fantasies to enlarge their vision and reality."

"So, why do you play Afrobeat, the quintessential music of protest, every day of the year?"

"Protest is only one of its aspects. At the core is a philosophy of life. But, really, I play *Baba's* Afrobeat because he is the greatest. I used to tell my lecturers that the Shrine is the new Egypt of African civilization."

"Haile! No wonder you didn't make it. But a BA Attempted like you should not wall himself in with such mighty rocks, I keep telling you. Have you learned nothing? Perhaps I should be happy you're playing 'White Christmas' this year; it's a sign that you're not irredeemably lost. But look around you, Haile, look around you; evil is on the loose."

From his residence in Coconut Island, Ashikodi, a habitué of Prinzi's Café, expounded his own views on Haile's "White Christmas" immersion. The island was home mainly to fishermen from diverse countries on the West Coast of Africa and was so called because it had once been a forest of coconuts. If indeed they had flourished there, the coconuts had since been replaced with shanties, fishing stations, and shrines. The place was famous for the hedonism of its residents, a near-exclusive tavern for sailors, and a sensual Communion of the Long Tide – an annual, orgasmic event to conclude the main fishing season.

In his early years of settling there, not much was heard of Ashikodi – who, like Haile, had also studied History but who, unlike him, had graduated. He had busied himself establishing a livestock farm, and it was not until he had nurtured it to the point of contracting out the management that he transformed into "the troubler of Coconut Island," as he was sometimes rather fondly described because of his idiosyncrasies. His skills for headwalking and ventriloquism became manifest and, when he discovered

Prinzi's Café on one of his tours, he felt he had finally found an "altar." He became a regular visitor to Maroko, so much so that he was soon accepted as a non-resident "Maroko person."

That Christmas season, however, he declared a "boycott" of Maroko, preferring instead to carouse in the island tavern for sailors – mostly expatriate semi-nomads who stopped by to check out the local flesh market. "That Haile and his ahistorical bunkum, I don't want his blood on my head. I believe I'd be tempted to smash his head, false dreadlocks and all, if I were to go to Maroko. 'White Christmas' indeed! A modern-day extension of 'Rule Britannia'! The smell of the ocean, he doesn't even know, is the very smell of God. He seeks in far-flung esoterica that which is all around him. Poor Maroko, what an affliction to bear – in these times!"

Two

Death was on the loose in New Maroko that season. Ignatius was the first to go. Ignatius the Hunchback. A beefy fellow with agitated eyes and the tattoo of a fish on his usually clean-shaven head, he would make jokes and arresting remarks about his hump: "It's not the fault of the hunchback that he carries on him the secrets of all the earth. That is what is locked away in the vaults of the hump. When I walk down the street, does the hump not speak to you? The hump is the voice of God!"

He had appeared in Maroko one dawn with an unforgettable story of being on land exile. "The mysteries of the river are as deep as its bottom," he had pronounced, and the fact that he had until recently been a canoeist had lent weight to his words. "I used to transport people across the Niger. 'Come on board, come on board, the Hump will take you there. Money back guarantee in case of accident.' Nothing like a money back guarantee, even an improbable one, to draw customers. I had the most fetching canoe for miles around – I had modeled it after a ship, can you imagine that? – and there were days I had to select my passengers amidst the rush to get on board. And I knew the river. My father and his father before him and my father's father's father had all been canoeists. And let me tell you, the river is not just water flowing; it is a flux of depths upon depths.

"So, when one morning a dashing, young woman came up to board my canoe, I was in two minds whether to take her. There was something about her that set off alarm bells in my ancient brain. You see, the river never claims what does not belong to it. But the river that rejects is also the river that passionately, even implacably, claims its own. When I saw this dashing, young woman – saw the look in her eyes, noted her ankle chain and her build – I said to myself: 'Ignatius, you know the river. Is she not of the river?' But she pleaded with me. She had to get to Ahaba within the hour. Her pleas melted my hardening heart, and I rowed off with her on board.

"Right in the middle of the river, it happened. The water rose in great heaves, obviously intent on capsizing my canoe. But why is the hunchback a hunchback if the vaults of his hump are empty of the secrets of the earth and the rivers? I knelt down in my canoe and called the river by its seven secret names, and I put out my hand to touch the waves and I pleaded with the spirit of the Niger: 'It's me, Ignatius, Ignatius the Hunchback. Between us, there is no schism. But you know the children of these days; they know nothing, although *nothing* knows them. Allow us this safe passage, this one time.' But the waves rose higher and higher. Another moment and all would have been lost 'O spirit of the Niger,' I cried out once more, 'if you let us pass through this one time, I will sacrifice to you a whole goat and I will chasten myself with three years of exile.' The rage of the river subsided, and I rowed like never across its expanse. I had gained a safe passage, but I had also lost my livelihood.

"The sacrifice was not easy. A whole goat is not a cockroach. But I had made a pact with the river. So, the next day, at the hour of flux between the night and the day, I cast the promised goat into the water. When it was washed ashore, its head was gone. Afterward, I set out on the road of life and it led me – a denizen of the river – to Maroko. I am a canoeist on exile, which is why I have scraped off my hair and tattooed a fish on my head. But the river is in my blood, and to it I shall return in due course."

He had spent three years in Maroko before the compelled relocation to New Maroko, off the coast of the Atlantic Ocean. Ignatius had been one of the first to arrive. He had transformed himself from an odd-jobber to a fisherman and soon became known all over for his prize catches. He had already garnered so many unofficial laurels that when the New Maroko Fishing Festival was announced, it was interpreted as a launching event for the formal crowning of Ignatius the Hunchback.

Shanka, a wily character who had been the leader of the hunters' guild in Maroko and who had surfaced in New Maroko barely six months ago, made the announcement. With no hill to hunt in in the new settlement, Shanka had set up "in business." No one knew precisely what Shanka did these days, but there was ample evidence that whatever it was was flourishing. When he went about announcing the fishing festival "to inaugurate the Christmas season and the anniversary of the exodus," not many paid him any great attention. But when he announced the prime prize of a cow and had the animal paraded around the settlement, New Maroko at last began to bustle with preparations.

The competition was fierce. Many were the contestants. Few were the rules. "Just get into the water – on foot, on canoe or whatever – and haul out the biggest fish. If the scale here says so, you go home with the cow," Shanka announced to the contestants and the spectators, many of whom had come to New Maroko especially to witness the event.

"Ashikodi, look after that cow for me," Ignatius called out with supreme confidence before he rowed off in his ship-like canoe, his clean-shaven head gleaming in the sun as if it had just been oiled. Although his exile was over, he had taken to keeping his head that way. "What is the worth of a tattoo buried underneath a forest of hair?" he would say. "And what is memory without its tattoo?"

Ashikodi was Ignatius's closest friend. The two had met the week Ignatius turned up in Maroko. Ashikodi had offered him a place to sleep in his Coconut Island residence, an arrangement that had lasted until Ignatius secured a room of his own in Maroko. The two were often seen together, although while Ignatius evidently had a passion for work, Ashikodi appeared to have developed an aversion to it. Ignatius had also studied History, via a correspondence college, but only enough to earn an associate degree.

When a shout was raised far out in the water, not many of the spectators understood whether it was one of triumph or alarm. When they saw a ship-like canoe buck up like a flying boat before capsizing, however, the cloud of doubt cleared. Even as the other canoes converged around the one in distress, rescuers launched off from the beach in standby canoes. Eventually, the canoe was towed back to the waterfront, but the whereabouts of its owner remained unknown. The explanatory tales grew big heads and long tails. Some said Ignatius the Hunchback had been swallowed by a big fish he had attempted to haul in. A fierce fight had ensued between him and the fish and, although he had fought valiantly, he had eventually lost to its greater might. Others swore the tattoo on his head had suddenly become a real fish-dragon and had sucked him into the belly of the water with emissions of fire. Some there were who reported that the hunchback had actually caught a prize fish and had hauled it in but had simultaneously vaporized, his hump disappearing first. Shanka announced that the competition had been canceled and that the cow would be slaughtered, after the period of mourning, and shared among the people in honor of "the Hump who would have been Champ." His legend began to grow.

"The Lord has given and the Lord has taken away; blessed be the name of the Lord," Ashikodi intoned at the funeral. That season, after the death of Ignatius the Hunchback, he was overflowing with biblical pronouncements. When he was not blessing the name of the Lord for giving and taking away, he chanted: "Blessed are the merciful for they shall receive mercy, blessed are the pure in spirit for they shall see God."

"Hey, what are you talking about?" challenged Haile when Ashikodi burst into his shop one evening muttering his new incantation.

"How can the Hump not see the god of killer fishes now?" he returned and continued on his way.

In Prinzi's Café, he recounted a dream vision in which Ignatius the Hunchback was a prince living away from home. "He was the Hump Prince or Prince Hump, whichever. And then his father, the king, died. The kingmakers sent him a message to come home and ascend his father's throne. 'Go tell them,' he said to the messenger, 'my kingdom is not of this world.' But that same day, he went mad. His people were bothered. They now had no king and their prince was mad in exile. So, they went to the river and pleaded with the water spirit to save them – in return for a commensurate sacrifice. When she appeared to the Hump Prince as a dashing, young woman, he could not resist her; she seduced him and enticed him homeward. The moment he set foot in his homeland, he became well again. But the water spirit had fallen in love with him and, instead of taking him to his people, took him into the depths of the river. In frustration, his people put a goat with the tattoo of a fish on its forehead on the throne and called it King Ignatius."

The tale created a disquieting stir in the café, but Ashikodi was gone before the patrons could gather themselves together.

"You see what I mean?" cried Prinzi. "The best novels are not always the ones written. That little fellow is a fantastic author..."

"Too many little heads and little fellows in your imagination, Prinzi. You must be a miniaturist," said Razaki, a diminutive playwright resident in Tarzan Jetty – a sparsely populated beach resort close to Coconut Island – but often to be found at Prinzi's Café.

"You know, sometimes, the smaller a thing is the more poetic. Have you not noted that in fables?"

Goomsi was the second to go. He died on the day of Ignatius's funeral. Once the major-domo at the Maraki Palace in Maroko, the forced relocation had cost him that job. He had then irritably moved from one odd job to the other – until the train accident that finally punctuated his strivings. The circumstances that had led to his fleeing Goom Station, his hometown in Ghana, was one of the well-known stories in Maroko.

"If I had stayed back there, my pieces would have since rotted under the ground. The place must be cursed. The train station was its heartbeat, but the rail was also the mangler that dispatched my father and my elder brother. My father was a train driver. However, it was neither the train nor the rail that was dear to him; it was Schnapps. He would sit on the veranda after the day's work drinking Schnapps and bemoaning his station in life. 'This is not what I planned for myself, boy,' he would say to me as if also speaking to the sky. 'A cocoa plantation and a beach house, yes, certainly not a stilted hut without electricity. In my lifetime, I have seen Goom degenerate from a promising town, hence your name, to a station for the dead. I don't suppose you properly understand what I'm talking about, boy, but at least you've got a brain. Use it. The trains used to arrive and depart from here with such regularity that our hearts beat in tune with the motion. Those days, boy, our hearts really beat! There was work for everybody and the traffic held out all sorts of promise. But, today, the big lorry-owners have conspired with their political *sinfants* in government to corner the freight business and derail the trains. And Goom Station has become a ghost town. You still wonder why I drink Schnapps so much? Because then it all comes back to me, including my cocoa plantation and beach house. My Schnapps never fails.' And he would take a generous gulp sure to get him coughing and sputtering and ranting. Then, one day, without warning, he leaped out of the train. Such a small distance, such a smash. The medicine man consulted his beads and declared that he must have willed the smash for it to have happened at all, and so terribly at that. We buried him and carried on with our lives. But we could as well have been our own pallbearers.

"The next year, a speed train crushed my elder brother in the same area. He was a strange one, my elder brother – not much unlike Ashikodi. Strange and deaf. No one ever found out what he was doing at the unlit rail tracks at that time of the night, or how the accident happened. Besides the gory death, I was particularly troubled by the fact that it was he who had brought the news of our father's death and I was the one who found his own body. It seemed very much like an unwanted relay to me. I was returning from my night shift in the darkness of a typical Goom Station dawn – there, dawn comes in gloomful gray – when my feet struck the bundle of flesh and bones. With the light from my torch, I examined that horrible discovery and then ran home to wake up people to come and help gather the pieces together for a burial. I knew then, even without the medicine man saying so, that if I stayed on in that accursed Doom Station, I would be the next victim. So, I gathered my things and fled – until the road led me to Maroko."

Life, which had been relatively kind to him in Maroko, had become very mean after the exodus, and gradually Goomsi had resigned himself to begging for a living. In the beginning, he just begged. "Help the poor, brother." "Can you help a distressed brother, sister? God bless you. Your womb will never be barren." But, on many occasions, he could as well have been speaking to the air. So, he had taken to feigning injuries or gumming up his eyes and acting the blind man tapping his way through life. His fortune did not improve much. His desire to become "a gentleman beggar" began to be heard with increasing stridency.

On the night he died, he had braced himself for the "operation" called "Maroko surgery" that transformed the destitute into "proper beggars." He had waited for the train by the rail tracks and then stuck out a leg just as the train rolled by him. But he had miscalculated and the train had almost severed his entire lower region. The train had stopped and he had been rushed to the General Hospital, but the injury was fatal.

Shanka took the responsibility for arranging the burial – beside the grave of Ignatius the Hunchback in the New Maroko cemetery. "'Let the dead bury the dead.' So it is written in the Bible, but if the living don't bury the dead, they too will soon be requiring a burial themselves," he said when asked about his new role as the community's undertaker.

"Is it fitting and proper that those whom the gods love should die young and set their people against their gods?" Ashikodi intoned at the funeral. "Is it not fitting and proper that those whom the gods love should die young so that their people will remember their gods?" It became his new inquiry. At Prinzi's Café, he recounted a dream vision in which Goomsi was a train-stopper at Goom Station. "Somehow, the trains will no longer stop at Goom Station, so the people employ Goomsi to stop the trains. He has a well-appointed office opposite the tracks and a billowing uniform – an impressive windcheater. When the train-sighter gives him the signal – 'Goomsi, the train cometh, Gentleman Goomsi!' – Goomsi will saunter out of his office and point a finger at the train or nod at it and the train will promptly grind to a halt. He becomes such an adept that they even put out posters announcing his act as a tourist attraction. Then, the trains grow stubborn and will no longer obey him; so, he begins to step in front of them and stop them with his body. He will leap up and do an acrobatic dance in the air and then stop the train with his back. The people set up a Gentleman Goomsi Tourist Board and begin to charge fees for the act. They also invent a song:

> "'Come and see
> Goom Station wonder
> Come and see
> Goom Station wonder
> Goom Goom Goom
> Goom Goom Goom
> Goom Station wonder'

"The trains become even more defiant and Goomsi begins to feel the impact of metal on flesh. But he is already a star, so he can afford all sorts of doctors. His audience demands variety, so he accepts to do the Leg Show once more. But the train has firmly developed other ideas. When Goomsi sticks out his leg at the train, wriggling his upper region to the chant of 'Goom Station wonder,' the train does not stop; it gores him like a bull savaging a matador's career and continues on its way. Goomsi appears to have perfected his magic; he metamorphoses into a bullet train and, in one blaze of destruction, knives through Goom Station. The remnants rename the town Goomsi – in an attempt to appease his spirit."

"By God," cried Prinzi, by which time Ashikodi had vanished, "this 'Roko is something!"

"Perhaps you'll do well to collect his dream visions. You know, *Ashikodi's Dream Visions: Short tales collected and introduced by Prinzi*," said Razaki.

"My friend, no more short stories for Prinzi. The short story is the solace of failed novelists."

"Prinzi! You know, you're guilty of the same thing you accuse Haile – extravagant convictions. Can't you see that the short story is the genre of the future? Don't you see the difference between the wonders of the Ancient World and those of the modern era?"

"Your convenient examples don't impress me. The world is so old and scarred that there are convenient examples for virtually everything. But that Ashikodi, the hawker of strange dream visions, the next time he comes here with one of his tales, someone has to stop him. It's even strange the way he's been acting, considering that he's one of the Seven Fingers."

"I hope he doesn't come with another such tale, because that would mean another death has occurred."

An unanswered wish. Madam Bonus was the third to go. She was the proprietress of the Bonus Club, a brothel known for its buxom women and unique invitation: "Pay for ten tumbles, have one free." She was also a patroness of beggars and usually held a Sunday luncheon for them. But it was not for either of these reasons that she was best known. It was for her phenomenal ability as a drinker.

"Madam Bonus? She can drink anyone under the ground. I've never seen her match anywhere."

"She must have spent a long time in hell before this incarnation. Why else would she be so thirsty?"

So, when Madam Bonus passed out during a drinking competition and never recovered, New Maroko gasped with astonishment. Many remembered the story the woman often told about the circumstances that had led to her fleeing her parents' home. She had just turned eighteen at the time and was concluding her A level studies. Her ambition was to study music in the university – like her idol, Fela – but she dared not mention the idea to her parents. And they made it clear enough that they could not afford to send her to the university.

"My father was a bricklayer in Bayangari. My mother had ten of us – all boys, except me. They reckoned that my bride price would ease the financial pressure on the family – at least, for some time. The first man they brought home to marry me was a prosperous contractor who already had three wives. I nicknamed him 'No Froblem' because of his speech mannerism. '*Mallama*,' he would say to me, 'I have frought you some *kilishi*. You know *kilishi*, *ba*? Good meat, flenty of iron, flenty of frotein. Once you marry me, *mallama*, no froblem at all at all.' I didn't want him and I made that clear. I played Afrobeat secretly and my world grew larger and headier.

"When my parents tired of forcing No Froblem on me, they brought home 'Dollar, Pounds.' He was ahead of his time in a sense. The naira was as strong as the dollar in those days, so his claim that he was 'dollar rich and pounds wealthy' did not impress me. But he had style. He showered me with gifts, which my parents promptly confiscated. What really got to me were the vistas he opened up. He would take me shopping in New York, tanning – can you imagine that? – in London, dining in Rome, sightseeing in Paris. I was moved in spite of myself, and looking back now I sometimes wish I had married him. This life! But then there were two obstacles: he already had one wife and he believed in the purdah system. Could I, at least, go to the university and study...anything at all? '*Haba, mallama*,' he would exclaim. 'University not good at all for women. University spoil women.' He spoke almost like a telegram, but he was honest. I rejected him too and threatened to take an overdose of sleeping tablets. For a time, my parents left me alone.

"Unknown to me, however, they had collected my bride price without letting out a word. When my father's fortune suddenly improved and he opened a grocery store for my mother and bought a taxi for himself, I cheered with all my heart that at last I had been saved by fate. *Ina*? When the school closed and they arranged for me to visit a distant uncle whom I had never heard of before then, in Kano, I was excited. I wanted to get away for some time. And I was to travel by air. The thrill alone beclouded whatever suspicion I might have had. A handsome but elderly man met me at the airport and introduced himself as my uncle. Everything went well until after I had retired for the night. He came into my room and reintroduced himself as my husband. And he raped me. It took me a very long week to escape from that house.

"Once out of that hell, I had only one destination: 'Kalakuta Republic,' the kingdom of *Baba* himself. It had always been a secret dream of mine, and I had nowhere else to go anyway.

"I learned to drink and dance, and it did not take long before I became one of *Baba's* 'wives.' I learned a lot in Kalakuta, and I did get to tour the world. It was a different kind of fulfillment, but I had a good time. Then came that day when aggrieved soldiers stormed the 'republic' and razed it to the ground, bulldozing and raping their way through. It was time to leave, a decision I had almost arrived at before that time. Life is like a ladder. You climb one rung, another looms; you fulfill one wish, another beckons. With Segi's mother, who was my best friend at Kalakuta, I came to Maroko, and one thing led to another until we set up the Bonus Club. As you know, she died at childbirth and Segi became my daughter."

Segi was the toast of New Maroko. Both the enchanting dancer at the Bonus Club as well as its manager, she was seen as unusually virtuous. She it was who usually strove, with infrequent success, to moderate Madam Bonus's drinking. On the night Madam Bonus died, Segi had protested vigorously when she began a drinking competition with three others.

"Now, I'm going to show you boys some real drinking. If I win, you get a free drink. If you win, you get a free tumble. There's always a bonus at the Bonus Club."

"Not today, madam," protested Segi. "You've drunk a brewery already in one lifetime and you know what the doctor said the last time you were in hospital."

"Since when do I need a doctor, who may not even be better than Centigrade, to regulate my life?"

"But, madam..."

"Segilola!"

Segi it was who arranged for her to be taken to hospital when she slumped halfway through the second bottle. She it was too who saw to the subsequent funeral, although Shanka offered his assistance.

"You hear say Shanka don volunteer to do Madam Bonus burial with his own money?"

"Eh, but Segi no 'gree. And I no blame am. The woman be like her own mama, and money no really be her problem. No be like Ignatius and Goomsi."

"My own mind be say: which kin' sympathetic undertaker Shanka don become? Since when the man surface for New Maroko – only im know where e go wey e come learn to speak in slow motion – e dey do like say im be angel of mercy."

"That one dey pain you?"

"E dey make me wonder. Why e be say im never help that im Epi Eye girlfriend wey still dey do *ashawo* for Good Evening Hotel yonder?"

"Shanka dey try. No how wey person go do make e satisfy this world."

"Na you know. Me, until I chop the man money, I go still take one eye dey look am."

Madam Bonus's funeral was the biggest New Maroko had ever witnessed. Ashikodi was there, and in between his incantation of what he called "the elastic chain of the dead" – "Dodos: ashes to ashes. Atlantis: flux to flux. Bonus: earth to earth" – he sang with passion:

> Abide with me
> Fast falls the eventide
> The darkness deepens
> Lord with me abide

"Gone, the Bonus from the Bonus Club," he chanted the next day at Haile's Record Shop. At Prinzi's Café, he recounted a dream vision in which Madam Bonus was swimming through a river of alcohol. "The farther she swims, the farther the shore recedes. Finally, in a fit of anger, she begins to drink her way through. By the time she gets to the shore, she has drunk the river dry. As she begins to walk home, the drips from her body transform into a river of crystal-clear water. The more the men drink, the more they are aroused. Each night, a long queue forms in front of Madam Bonus's door, but she will only take in three men. One night, however, compassion seizes her at the sight of so many seekers, and she decides to accommodate the entire queue. So, from dusk to dawn, the men file in and out of her room until, with the last man, she finally reaches a grand orgasm. Then, she acquires wings and flies skyward in her fleshy nakedness."

Prinzi had positioned himself by the door and effectively stopped Ashikodi from vanishing as usual. "Now, sit down, the 'Roko," he invited, nudging him into a chair, "have a drink on the house and tell us how you come by these strange tales. And why have you been playing tell-and-vanish with us?"

"I dream, therefore I am. I am, therefore I dream," said Ashikodi. "I speak, therefore I vanish. I vanish, therefore I speak."

"Well spoken, but how does that educate anybody? How come you are the only one having these dreams and seeing these visions – and with such punctuality?"

"What is the dream vision but reality renewed?" said Ashikodi, then he summoned his ventriloquistic ability and began to speak from different corners of the room: "Gone, the Chump from the Hump, the Station from Goom, the Bonus from the Bonus Club."

"The 'Roko speaks," Razaki said drily.

"Can you teach me how to do that?" Shanka, who was present at the café that night, asked Ashikodi. "I'll pay you handsomely."

"*You* will *pay* Ashikodi? Very interesting. I wish I could assist you, but it can't be taught. It's a genetic inheritance of the Ashikodis of this world."

"Is it, really? I thought that with some special voice training..."

"No, it's strictly genetic. V.I.P. – Voice in Paradise. I think there's a special committee of angels, headed by Gabriel of the Immaculate Conception fame, in charge of the gift. Maybe a direct petition will work in your favor. I can help with the postage."

Amidst the ensuing laughter, which had Prinzi and Razaki rocking on their feet, Ashikodi began a new demonstration of his ventriloquism. Shanka changed the topic.

"Ignatius drowned in the Atlantic. There was no ocean finger in Maroko. Goomsi died on the rail tracks. There were no rail tracks in Maroko. Madam Bonus choked to death on the second bottle. She used to drink two cartons at a sitting in Maroko. Something is amiss. Perhaps some of our spirits have not made or survived the journey from the old to the new."

"Perhaps."

"In one week, it'll be Christmas Eve – exactly one year we were bulldozed out of Maroko. I propose an all-night vigil, in the old Maroko, both to mark our survival and as a way of leading lingering spirits back to New Maroko."

The idea was enthusiastically enlarged by Razaki. "A ritual theater!" he exclaimed. "A first-rate idea."

"I will bear the cost," volunteered Shanka. "Prinzi, a drink for everyone. Madam Bonus would not want to be remembered with glum faces."

"This little Shanka fellow," Prinzi said to Razaki, after serving the drinks. "He disappears for six months, to a big secret of a destination, and when he reappears, he's become more Santa than Santa Claus."

"More princely than Prinzi."

"Oh, be serious. I have the feeling that he will eventually catapult himself to the center of the great Maroko novel. Something is afoot."

"Leave Shanka alone, Prinzi, and get on with this novel of yours. It's beginning to look as if it'll end up as the greatest novel never written."

"Not a chance. I'll start with this march. Quite striking, don't you think? I can see it clearly now – the first sentence: 'On the day it marched back to Maroko for the commemoration of its exodus, New Maroko went with a heart heavy with grief and remembrance but lightened by survival and hope.' What about that? Prinzian, isn't it?"

"Whatever happened to the beatitude of damnation and of survival?"

"A novel in progress progresses, my friend."

"Hey, Ashikodi," called Shanka from his corner. "Why don't you propose a toast, man?"

"To what?"

"Our survival, despite everything. To the future, to the stars yet to shine."

As if on cue, the music in Haile's Record Shop changed from an Afrobeat song to "White Christmas." *And may all your Christmases be white, Christmases be white.*

Three

On the day they marched back to Maroko, many residents of New Maroko went with hearts heavy with grief and remembrance but lightened by survival and hope. Shanka had worked hard to give the event life and had even talked Haile into playing "Sorrow, Tears and Blood" instead of "White Christmas."

"What happened?" Prinzi asked Haile.

"It's in honor of the dead. The spillage of their blood has caused sorrow and tears among us, has it not? Answer me that."

"Should gloom speak to gloom then? Do the people of the slum no longer need melody and fantasy?"

"Oh, come off it, Prinzi. Ignatius the Hunchback. Goomsi. Madam Bonus. And all those who died on the day the earthmovers erased Maroko. Is the litany of our dead not long enough?"

"There's the story making the rounds that Shanka had to buy several records and make other commitments to win you over to your new mood?"

"What will the slum be without its tattles?"

"That sounds like an echo of Ashikodi's 'What will libation be without wine?' Now, you answer me that."

"What then will the slum be without its tattles and echoes? I do know that Jah abideth with me."

"Parables to parables, eh? Well, thanks to Shanka, I notice you come in here often these days. Another beer? Yes, that's the spirit, my friend."

"Why does everybody suddenly see Shanka in everything?"

"Because he is, suddenly, in everything. Tell me: how's the Shrine these days? Do you still feel at home there?"

"Of course. Even in the Shrine, I sometimes hum 'White Christmas.' The new Egypt is also a new diffusion."

Both Prinzi and Haile were part of the march that Christmas Eve. Razaki was at the front. Shanka, also at the fore, had seen to it that each person in the procession that now snaked out of New Maroko had a white candle and a candleholder, "courtesy of Kaabiyesi Investments." He had promised each one a chunk of meat from the cow he said would be slaughtered on their return – in honor of the "hump who would have been champ." He had also talked up the march.

"We will go back to Maroko in remembrance of where we came from – were driven from, as a matter of fact – and to appease whatever spirits remain to be pacified. It is time. This cycle of death must cease."

"And what will we do when we get there?"

"We will ring the old marketplace and hold a candlelight vigil. We will perform some sacrifices and sing until Christmas morning."

"What sacrifices, and who will provide them?"

"Fowls and goats. I will provide everything that is required, on behalf of Kaabiyesi Investments."

Since the death of Madam Bonus, Shanka had taken to announcing that he was acting on behalf of Kaabiyesi Investments. The death of the proprietress of the Bonus Club was not, however, the explanation for this new mannerism. Two days after the burial of Madam Bonus, New Maroko had been roused in the early hours of the morning by the arrival of Kaita, "the Kaita of Kaabiyesi Investments" as Shanka described him. Attired in a flamboyant *buba* and *sokoto*, he rode on a white stallion with a black mane. He was trailed by four horsemen and preceded by a long line of cars. A trumpeter heralded the picturesque arrival.

With the mouth of New Maroko open in wonder, the party made its way through the awakened streets to a little-known corner of the settlement where a palace appeared to have been built overnight. It was an impressive house with massive doors and spectacular colonnades. A wall plastered with murals virtually shrouded the house. On the gate was a sign that proclaimed: Kaita Palace.

The approach of the party was welcomed with a twenty-one-gun salute, with Shanka superintending the shooters. That evening and at mealtimes every day afterwards, steaming basins were set up outside the gate and food generously dished out to the needy. As the people now marched back to the past, they also talked about Kaita Alhaji Kaita and his grandiloquent palace, which Shanka had named "The Palace of Good."

"That Alhaji Kaita is quite a man, I tell you. Remark how he has taken the poor of New Maroko as his people. This country certainly needs more philanthropists like him, more Palaces of Good."

"Probably so, but who is he and where did that exclamatory house of his spring from in these lean times? Every morning, he is chauffeured to the office of Kaabiyesi Investments, but what exactly does the company do? And his wife and children, are they real at all? One hardly ever sees or hears them."

"You see the problem with questions. You ask one and you have to ask another, until you begin to lose yourself in the maze. What do you mean by who the man is? He is a Nigerian obviously, and evidently a good one. As for the house, its so-called 'sudden appearance' only shows up our poor knowledge of our not-so-new settlement. I did notice signs of construction down there but somehow never took an abiding or even imaginative interest. And what do you expect from Kaabiyesi Investments? To hawk bread or meat or sugar on the streets to show that it is genuine?"

"Since when did a question become an answer to a question? If you know so much, tell me the meaning of the murals on his walls – lions eating goats, funeral processions, and such."

"Those are images of nature. I suspect the man must be an environmentalist. Consider the landscaping around Kaita Palace. I'm sure he is in communion with the various forms of nature."

"You're beginning to sound like Shanka."

"And why not? Shanka is a first-rate fellow, a new John the Baptist."

"So, Alhaji Kaita is the new Christ of Maroko, eh? What blasphemy!"

"So it might seem at first."

"Anyway, where's the man gone to? I understand he traveled yesterday – with people showering his car with confetti."

"I was one of those people. First, he visited the cemetery, to lay wreaths on the graves of Ignatius the Hunchback, Goomsi, and Madam Bonus, then he stopped near the Bonus Club where he planted a tree and promised to build an Anniversary Square to commemorate our first year here."

"And afterward?"

"I understand he's traveled to the capital on business. You don't stay in one spot to watch a big masquerade, and the big masquerade does not stay in one spot to perform."

At the fore of the procession, Prinzi asked Razaki: "What do you think of Alhaji Kaita?"

"He strikes me as an actor in the wings awaiting his cue."

"Come on, my friend, the man is already here, so what are you talking about?"

"I notice you haven't begun to refer to him as a little fellow and do not sound likely to start, at least not anytime soon."

"Wouldn't that be overstating the case? But, come on, can't you see the man has already taken the center stage?"

"The man is here, yes, but do you believe he came here to minister to the hungry? That's a smoothening process for something that will benefit Kaabiyesi Investments and its principals."

"You know, you can be deep sometimes," Prinzi said with a mischievous smile.

"Don't give me that tongue of yours this morning."

"You want my balls instead?" Prinzi said and roared into laughter. "I think you're right," he added later. "A man like Alhaji Kaita, who rides a white horse and can spring a palace of a surprise, is miscast in the role of an altruist. He's either working up to something or maybe working on it already, with the active connivance of a mask like Shanka."

Meanwhile, Shanka was everywhere, urging the people on.

"I tell you, people, this return is also a journey into the

future – a golden age of bountiful pleasures. To Caesar his due, to God his, and to us too. I have Alhaji Kaita's word that he will turn New Maroko into a New Paradise, after we have cleansed the land and ourselves. And as you all know, Alhaji Kaita Alhaji is a man of his word."

As the procession was about to leave New Maroko behind, Shanka called a halt. "Here is where New Maroko meets the outside world," he said, "so let the sacrifice begin here."

"What for?" asked a few voices.

"To bid farewell forever to evil spirits dogging our footsteps and to bar their access to New Maroko forevermore."

"And in Maroko?" inquired fewer voices.

"There, we will entreat all the good spirits left behind to make the transition with us and compel insistent evil spirits still dogging our steps to make their homes there."

Under Shanka's supervision, a goat and some fowls were slaughtered at the exit from New Maroko and prayers said to diverse deities. The procession was about to start marching again when Ashikodi, who had been unusually quiet all along, insisted on leading a prayer session.

"Let us pray in the name of God," he said.

"In the name of God? What other God?" protested one of the marchers.

"If you don't know, I will tell you," Ashikodi retorted. "That's the problem with you Maroko people. Death is all around you, yet you argue about the name of God. If you don't know, I will tell you!" And he began to scream: "Ismoog! Sunob! Suitangi! These are the names of God in New Maroko this year and the next."

"Ashikodi, we all know how much you loved the Hump," Prinzi tried to placate him, "but how does a reversal of his name, and those of Madam Bonus and Goomsi, translate into the name of God?"

"Death reversed is life. Life is light. God is light."

"Look here, God is not a mental exercise," said Haile.

"Let's move on, people. He can pray all day if he wants to."

Shanka made peace by appealing for tolerance. "Ashikodi is one of us, people. If he wants to say special prayers according to his understanding, why not?"

When the tumult had subsided, Ashikodi astounded everyone by walking on his head in circles and shrilling "Ismoog! Sunob! Suitangi!" ventriloquially. The performance was so good that many in the crowd clapped afterward and the procession continued in lighter spirits.

Beyond New Maroko, beyond other similar settlements, the road finally broadened out into the streets of Greater Lagos. For many of the marchers, the streets and the buildings – their workplaces, the dilapidated cinemas, the gargantuan stadium, the numerous churches – provoked memories and thoughts.

"See, Orita, them dey build another big stadium opposite this one. You see this country and the wickedness of these government people?"

"The two stadiums sef na so so thief thief. If contractor buy something one naira, he go claim say na one pound sterling, him and ministry people go share the surplus. Still, that one no do them. When they don build the thing finish, they go steal everything wey dey inside, then the government go give them maintenance contracts."

"Na stadium own you dey talk? See the roads as them be. When the roads dey damage small small, everybody go comot eye – until they don damage to reach billion-naira contract. Africa! One day, all of us go take head dey waka."

"Like Ashikodi?"

"Ah, Ashikodi no be anyhow person, no mind the kin' *wahala* wey e dey make sometimes. That one na im destiny."

"See how Rex Cinema don become like old woman wey dey carry walking stick dey waka. Before before, Rex na where the whole world dey come see magic. That time, the gateman sef dey dress like Central Bank governor. Now, see the man as e be like fowl wey rain don beat tire."

"Now sef, na only those old Indian films wey them dey sing 'pinya pinya pinya' na im them dey show. And that no be the only *wahala* sef. If you wan' go there these days, you get to carry bandage, because if they break one head for film inside, all these *agbero* people go break two outside."

"You think say their head still correct, with all the corner-corner hairstyle them dey call European Chanfer or American Hide and Seek?"

"Leave Rex Cinema first. Look Shelling Hotel. If you know the number of plates and cutlery wey I wash there, I reach to get chieftaincy title. But, my brother, nothing nothing. Na so so aroma. All these big men get long throat no be small."

"Na only their throat long?"

"Ah, Shelling Hotel no be Shelling Hotel for nothing-o. Na here all those big people wey don learn to speak in slow motion dey shell themselves. The things wey my eye see, my brother, no be small thing-o. All these cash madams with body like rainbow, when you see them inside air-conditioned room on top bed, you go shake head. Sometimes sef, they know man pass ordinary *ashawo* for Maroko."

"Idi Baba! Talk true, you no shell for there?"

"Who dash monkey coat? No be to shell na im carry me come Lagos-o. If I come shell finish and my wife and children no see food eat, which kin' sense be that? Anyway, all that one na history. Man don peg for Devil's Island."

Now in the middle of the procession, Prinzi and Razaki were also engaged in a similar discussion. "Look at that!" exclaimed Razaki, indicating the Jehovah Jireh Church a little distance after Shelling Hotel. "Each time I pass here, this architectural marvel makes me begin to hope again."

"Hope?" wondered Prinzi.

"It's like a peep into the future. This is architecture ahead of its time. Look at the effect of the spectrum of lights on the glassy façade. Look at how the stepped elevation and the peaking roof create the effect of flotation."

"But what is the point of a building like this here except the now familiar proclamation that 'my God is not a poor God,' despite the poverty all around? It's as inharmonious as playing Beethoven or Handel in a cheap discotheque at a sawdust brothel."

"A brilliant architect should, while taking note of his environment and time, strive to transcend them."

"Now you're beginning to sound like Haile: 'Should gloom answer gloom?'"

Both men smiled at the familiar turn of the conversation. "Have you ever been inside that church?" Prinzi asked.

"I haven't. That might affect my admiration."

"I think you should try writing a play about a director who refuses to read the script he is working on."

"Have you been inside the church yourself?"

"You know me, I would go anywhere – at least once – in search of stories. Yes, I have. And I think you should too. The seating arrangement is something to behold. Perhaps somewhere in the Bible there's a line that says: 'Thou shalt sit according to thy tithes.' That's the practice in there."

Toward the rear of the procession, Haile and Ashikodi marched side by side.

"They say I've been bought over, body and soul, by Shanka," said Haile as the march turned into the road that led to Maroko.

"And that's a surprise to you?" Ashikodi asked as he lit yet another cigarette.

"Bought over to what?"

"If only we know, if only you know. Better watch out, Haller."

"I've told you to stop calling me that."

"Haile, Haller, Holler. What's the difference? Can there be a Haile without a Haller? And can Haller resound without a holler? Whoever must dine with Shanka these days should have a long spoon. The man is a hunter and will always be."

"How come you still live in Coconut Island if you're such

a sage?"

"World people! Well, it's been fittingly said that reason is the devil's harlot."

"That's the problem: too many people in the slums these days who don't belong there – like you, Razaki, Prinzi..."

"And you, Shanka, Kaita. What is the sum of three such plus three such?"

"You should go to a kindergarten for that. The problem is that you would see evil even in the wand of God."

"Does your god carry a wand?"

"Shanka and Kaita have done more for the people than all the banter and high-sounding nothings from you pseudo intellectuals."

"Let me ask you, H – that okay? Do you still go to the Shrine?"

"With your omniscience, you shouldn't need to ask," Haile said in a manner he hoped was cutting and moved away.

Ashikodi made his way towards Segi. In the black mourning dress she had taken to wearing since the death of Madam Bonus and with her clean-shaven head, she looked like an animated sculpture. Dangling from her neck was a large wooden cross. Unlike many of the other women, she was barefooted.

"I have told you this before," Ashikodi said to her. "No matter how hard you try not to, you'll always look beautiful. It's your destiny."

She managed a wan smile. "This is not the time for such talk, Ashikodi."

"My dear, it's Christmas tomorrow. Hurrah for Christ!" And he propelled himself into the air, with a fist thrust skyward. "Let the dead bury the dead, Segi. I have cried myself hoarse, better believe it, but after a point grief begins to be tedious."

"You're a poet, you know."

"That's the revelation awaiting its time. So, am I allowed now to come and knock on your door at the Bonus Club?"

"If anyone else had dared ask me that question, which is

unlikely, I would have scratched his eyes out."

"Praise the Lord!"

"Shut up!" she said severely, drawing inquiring glances and concerned questions.

The procession marched on. By now, the initial hundred or so people that set off from New Maroko had become more than a thousand men, women, and children. Many of them had joined the group in solidarity or out of curiosity or even for lack of a more exciting occupation that afternoon. Despite the conversations, the singing had continued, with Shanka as the song leader. As the procession began to approach Maroko, he began a victory song. The tempo of the march quickened.

The signs of Christmas were everywhere evident along the route – in the carols from roadside houses, in frontal decorations with twinkling lights, in robust goats either bleating or peeping from their tethered corners. Many of the marchers especially noticed the astounding changes that had occurred in the area around the once-famous Maroko market. Where shacks had once been a landmark had been transformed within one year by spectacular houses with names such as Villa Shinkafi, Glory Castle, Cloud Palace. As the marchers moved toward their destination, they also gasped along. Such was the collective astonishment at the confirmation of the tales some of them had previously derided.

And, finally, Maroko. The shock was so much that the procession halted, even without any signal from Shanka. It was as if the shantytown they once lived in had never existed. Erased from the face of the earth were the hovels, the gutters notorious for their stench and as a breeding ground for mosquitoes, and the roadside market that sometimes drew more flies than buyers. Erased too were all the cheap brothels and bars. What the people now saw was a self-announcing, almost immaculate New Queenstown in which the buildings were like competing chest thumpers. An inner city that had been nothing but shriveled buttocks and flabby breasts and tobacco-stained teeth had become a wondrous metropolis of robust posteriors and bulbous anteriors and gold-filled dentures.

It was not as if the men were entirely ignorant of the transformation. The scramble and partition of Maroko by the affluent was a well-known story. Some of the marchers had actually beheld the consequence before; most had heard of it. But if individually outside Maroko they had fumed against the government and its beneficiaries, now collectively confronted with the reality inside Maroko, the brazen dispossession sent shivers of rage down their spine. Shanka produced a microphone and turned to the crowd now on the verge of becoming a mob.

"My people," he addressed them. "Welcome to Maroko. Whether they name it New Queenstown or Queenstown Annex or whatever else, it will always be Maroko to us. There in the background is the hill where I used to hunt. And there – I can still see it – is Mama Badejo's kiosk where the best beancakes in the whole world were made. Here was Maroko. Here is still Maroko. Here will always be Maroko."

The crowd managed to cheer.

"When they drove us out, they used safety and development as excuses," Shanka went on. "One year later, we return, and what do we see? Development, yes, but for robbers and contractors. Development for leg flashers and praise singers. I, Shanka, on behalf of myself and Kaabiyesi Investments and on behalf of everyone here today, I spit on their development."

As he matched the words with action, the crowd gave vent to its emotion as well.

"But sheathe your anger, people. They are having their day; ours will come. And then..." With his right hand at his throat, he made a gesture of decapitation. The crowd burst into a momentous cheer, chanting "Shanka! Shanka!" The man now brought out a piece of paper and displayed it to the crowd.

"I have here a police permit for this march," he told them. "Let us keep it peaceful and not give the police any reason to piece our lives asunder. Our mission here today is simple but vital. We want the season of deaths to pass over us. We want New Maroko to radiate life and progress, more than Maroko did. I have Alhaji

Kaita Alhaji's words that, by the Christmas season next year, this shall come to pass. As you all know, Alhaji Kaita Alhaji is an honorable man. It's a pity he could not be here with us today. A situation arose that necessitated his absence, but he certainly is here with us in spirit. Now that we are here, we will make all due sacrifices and pray and watch until Christmas dawn. Everything we will require in the way of refreshment will be provided." He broke into a Christmas song about three ships that came sailing in on Christmas morning. The crowd sang along, ending the rendition with chants of "Shanka! Shanka!" and "Shanka for Maroko! Maroko for Shanka!"

Under his supervision, several goats and fowls were slaughtered by volunteer cooks. As the people began to settle down along the road for the vigil, the first confrontation came – in the form of well-dressed men flanked by uniformed security guards leading Alsatian dogs straining at their leashes. They were residents of New Queenstown. Walking up to Shanka, they demanded an explanation for the "commotion."

"We have a police permit for this vigil," Shanka replied, once more displaying the document. "We are former residents of this Maroko and, even though you have benefited from our adversity, we mean no one any harm."

"You better get out while you still can," fumed the leader of the group. "The police have already been contacted and will be here shortly; then, you may not be able to get off so easily. Your congregation here, especially at this time of the day, is unacceptable."

"We will wait for the police," Razaki responded.

Wailing sirens announced the coming of the police – in several trucks. Leaping out of the trucks even before they screeched to a halt and fanning out with leveling rifles, the policemen stilled all talk between New Maroko and New Queenstown.

Calmly, Shanka displayed the permit to the leader of the riot squad – an Assistant Superintendent of Police. "This is our permit for this march and vigil," he said. "We mean no one any harm."

The man glared at the paper, then plucked it from Shanka's hand, tore it into shreds and fed the pieces to the evening breeze. "Your permit has been canceled. Now, you better do as Chief Ajayi here has requested and vanish from here."

For several moments, Shanka, Razaki, Segi, and all the other New Maroko notables looked speechlessly at the shreds of the permit.

"If I hadn't witnessed this, I would never have fully believed it," Prinzi said upon his recovery. "How can an ASP tear a permit issued by the Commissioner of Police? May we see your identity card, sir."

"You'll have to peruse your mother's nakedness first. In this place now, I am the Commissioner of Police. Move, or I will move you!"

"I have here with me a copy of the constitution," Ashikodi said and surprised everyone by producing the document. "Here, it guarantees us the right to peaceful assembly."

The ASP snatched the document from him and flung it away. "Now, where is your constitution? In this place now, I am the constitution. Your right to assembly is revoked."

"What kind of country is this?" wondered Haile.

"World people!" exclaimed Ashikodi.

In the ensuing tension, the women reshaped the confrontation. Mama Badejo was the first. Calmly, she removed her blouse and brassiere. One by one, several of the old women did the same, then they formed a mobile circle around the ASP, Chief Ajayi, Shanka, and all the other men.

"In my village," Mama Badejo addressed the police officer, "if an old woman like me utters a curse in her nakedness, there is no escaping it. Don't let us curse you in our nakedness."

It was the turn of the ASP – X277789, according to his number tag – to be dumbfounded.

"Look here, mama," Chief Ajayi said with unexpected softness, "no one is cursing anyone or asking to be cursed.

Tomorrow is Christmas, a time of joy all over the world. How would you feel if a crowd gathered outside your window with candles and knives?"

"But we have come in peace."

"Then peace be unto you, and to us as well."

By now, the women had begun a song – one that expressed the mood of the restive crowd:

>We no go 'gree-o
>We no go 'gree
>Police-o, we no go 'gree
>Queenstown-o, we no go 'gree
>Oga, comot for road
>We no go 'gree

"I have my orders," X277789 said ominously to Shanka. "For the last time, mister, I warn you: get your people out of here, or else their blood – and yours – will be on your head."

"We will leave at dawn. That is when our permit expires."

Turning to the group of well-dressed men and their dog handlers, X277789 said in his best Police Academy voice: "Chief Ajayi, I advise that you and your fellow gentlemen withdraw, so that we can deal with this rabble appropriately."

As Chief Ajayi and his group left, the police officer tried to rejoin his men, but the mobile circle of topless, old women had become a solid, singing wall.

Then something that shook everyone in the crowd happened. Most of the people had either heard of or even witnessed a demonstration by topless, old women. But only very few had heard of and almost no one had seen the presumably more deadly form of this sort of primal invocation – such a demonstration by a young woman. The surprise also stemmed from the fact that the demonstrator in this case was Segi, the toast of New Maroko. Removing her dress, she stood almost as naked as primal truth. She then walked toward the police officer – with a bearing that was also a rudimentary dance. The wall parted and she stood in front of X277789.

"In this place now, you are the government in power," she said to the stupefied man. "And in my nakedness, which Madam Bonus covered as long as she lived, I curse you."

As she burst into tears, the old women led her away.

Now released from the imprisoning wall, X277789 stumbled toward his men. Shanka began to rally the sobered crowd for a return to New Maroko. From somewhere in New Queenstown, the strand of a song fluttered in the dying breeze of a tropical evening: *Mary's boy child, Jesus Christ, was born on Christmas day.*

Four

Going back was harder. The procession of men, women, and children that left New Queenstown that Christmas Eve marched somewhat like a defeated army.

"What got into you back there?" Ashidodi asked Segi as they walked at the rear. "Your dance jolted all of us."

"Why? How many of the men have not seen me dance at the Bonus Club?"

"That is the difference between night and day, between the Bonus Club and the road that knives through Maroko. The timing and the environment condition the mind."

"Well, I think I danced for the same reason as the other women. Or maybe it was simply the madness of the moment."

"'The madness of the moment.' Prinzi will love that. He's like an Ignatius, a fisherman, casting his net far and wide for choice morsels of words to feed what I suspect must be a famished novel. The madness of the moment. I understand that – that moment when we lose our inhibitions and project our elemental selves in a bid to connect with the elemental forces of the universe and through ritual achieve that which reality denies us."

"Ashikodi! The madness of the moment is also the same as 'temporary insanity' often pleaded by murderers, rapists, and robbers."

"Now you're devaluing the phrase. But it's good we're talking, and I've noticed a smile almost illumine the beauty of your face. Don't suppress it. Words and laughter purge the soul."

Segi could not repress a smile this time. "All right, you do the talking and I'll do the listening," she said.

"Oh no, that's not the way to do it. A monologue isn't the same as a conversation."

"You're wasting your talents, I must say."

The two walked for some time in silence. Ashikodi lit a cigarette.

"You and this bad habit!" protested Segi. "Do you ever hear the warning that accompanies cigarette adverts: 'The Federal Ministry of Health warns that cigarette smoking is dangerous'?"

"I know that better than the impersonal Federal Ministry of Health. But it's Christmas tomorrow, Segi. Let's talk about something that will lift the spirit. Maybe we should sing a carol together. Hurrah for Christ! What do you say?"

"I really don't have fond memories of Christmas, except perhaps Christmas two years ago when I graduated from catering school. I was born during the Christmas season, and it wasn't a good time for any of us – especially my mother and Madam Bonus," she said sadly.

Ashikodi was touched. "Tell me all about it," he said. "Words purge the soul, remember?"

"You do say such memorable things." And she looked at him with a tenderness that propelled him into giddy heights. "At the time I was born, my mother and Madam Bonus had just arrived in Maroko, both drenched by the rain of ill fortune. Although Madam Bonus never told the story to anyone else, preferring instead to claim that they came straight to Maroko after the destruction of Kalakuta Republic, she and my mother traveled different roads before coming to Maroko. Both had fallen in love. My mother went to Badagry to get married to a Beninoise, my father. Unknown to her, the man was a polygamist and his house was a battlefront. Her arrival united all the other wives, four of them, against her. For all her naughtiness at the Shrine, my mother wasn't a fighter and she was soon vanquished. In any case, it must have been hell as a primipara, especially the thought of bringing up a child already branded a bastard in that sort of house.

"Madam Bonus was going through her own hell. She had moved in with her fiancé. The man's family was against the marriage, so they declared war on her – with *juju*, slander, and fisticuffs as armaments. A warrior, she gave as much as she got. Her fiancé railed against the gang-up, threw a few punches, and consulted a medicine man – all to no avail. When he could bear it no longer, he vanished. The family accused her of being responsible for his disappearance. She was arrested. When she was eventually released, she sought out my mother and together they came to Maroko – arriving in the week just before Christmas. Both had only enough money to rent a shack. That was how the Bonus Club began – somewhere near the Shit Lagoon, perhaps in the same spot that Pastor David built his church. And that was where I was born. My mother died in the process.

"If that first Christmas was bleak, so have been many others. In the early years, we were too poor for Christmas to matter. Even when our fortune changed, one quirk of fate after another ensured I had one bad Christmas after the other. There must be such a thing as a Christmas jinx. Perhaps my dance was really an act of exorcism."

"You're sui generis, Segi the Lola," Ashikodi said. To think you've endured so much sadness, yet you've always been enchanting."

"Come to think of it, how many people in Maroko can speak of Christmas with any fondness? You do remember the story of the old man who died in that terrible rain the first day the bulldozers tore down Maroko – the old man who, according to Shanka, must have died mouthing 'O come, all ye faithful'? I think he's the spirit of Christmas in Maroko."

"You make Christmas seem like an upper-class delicacy, Segi. It isn't about how many turkeys you eat or how much wine you quaff. It's a year-end season of reflection and fellowship."

"What will libation be without wine, remember?" she said with a smile.

"Ah, I s-e-e. Of course, that is true."

"For Maroko, Christmas will always be a season of gloom because of the eviction and now this disruption of a simple ceremony of remembrance and purgation."

"Sometimes, I don't bother much about my strivings amounting to anything. Who or what are we that we think we can reorder the mind of the universe? But such thoughts are for my sane moments. For Maroko, I have already pledged permanent insanity."

For the first time that day and perhaps since Madam Bonus's death, Segi actually laughed. An elated Ashikodi did a few dance steps despite the mood of New Maroko that Christmas Eve.

"Look that Ashikodi," Iya Idi said to Mama Badejo not far away. "Wetin don enter im head wey e dey dance for this kin' day?"

The march had entered the fabulous, tree-lined His Excellency Avenue in New Queenstown. Well-dressed children ran about injecting firecrackers primed for rainbows of detonation into the air. In front of the imposing St Christopher's Bakery, a sign announcing a ten percent discount for "Special Christmas Loaves" had been revised upward. From the interior of the Jehovah Jireh Church came the sound of the choir rehearsing "Noel." At one street intersection, there was an unsigned poster, recently put up, proclaiming: "To you the people of New Maroko: Merry Christmas and Happy New Year. To all men and women of goodwill: Greetings of the season." Toward the end of the avenue, where the procession had to turn into Sir Johnson Street, en route to the sprawling business district known as Greater Lagos, the traders selling turkeys and fowls at "bargain prices" were winding up with an air of satisfaction.

Although Iya Idi had been in the wall of women that ringed X277789, she had not dared shed her dress. Still not certain how her husband would respond to her limited participation in that protest, she had decided to keep her distance for as long as possible.

"You surprise say Ashidoki dey dance?" said Mama Badejo. "You no see say na im and Segi dey talk since? You know say Ashikodi get eye well well for where Segi dey."

"That Segi na wa-o. Wetin enter her head wey she begin dance like that?"

"Ah, e go be Madam Bonus spirit, wetin else? You know say Madam Bonus na strong woman and im and Segi dey like oil and pepper when she dey alive. Anyway, as e be say today be like say na Satan bless am for us, I no surprise for anything wey happen."

"I know that my redeemer liveth," Mama Badejo responded promptly. "But maybe God don forget us for this Maroko, *abi* New Maroko or whatever them dey call am. Me, I don make up my mind. I dey go back to my village."

"Which kin' talk be that? That one no be to jump from frying pan enter fire?"

"Na so me sef I been dey think. But I don see am finish today say nothing dey for this Lagos for people like us. All the time wey I dey my village before my husband carry me come Lagos, I no ever suffer like this."

"But, now, you don get children. Wetin una wan' do for village? Which kin' life you wan go back to – no job, no money, no electricity, no tap water, nothing."

"For Lagos *nko*? The same thing – no job, no money, no electricity, no tap water, nothing. And *orishirishi* Omo-ale full everywhere dey find whom they go slaughter. I dey carry all my children go my husband village. At least im people go help us small, we go help ourselves small, God go help us too. Iya Idi, na you be the first person wey I dey tell this: New Year no go meet us for Lagos."

"But this village matter no dey as you dey talk am-o. For village, na so so poverty, ghosts, gossip, backbiting..."

"Na true you dey talk, but the ones wey dey Lagos na them worse pass. Look, bush fowl and vulture no be the same thing. This village matter wey we dey talk so, you think say if no be the small village spirit wey we still get, we for never die or kill one another finish for Maroko? This dance wey we dance today, no be village spirit be that? Look, Iya Idi, I know that my redeemer liveth. I dey go meet am for village."

In the middle of the procession, Idi, Quiet, and Centigrade talked among themselves.

"That my wife, e be like say her ears need adjustment make she dey hear my word well well," complained Idi. "Wetin she come follow those women who surround that ASP dey do? Like say those certified killers wey them dey call mobile policemen begin shoot, wetin I for dey talk now?"

"You no happy say she no follow comot her dress..." began Quiet.

"Quiet, you! You no go go marry before the world completely pass you by?"

"Which kin' argument una wan start now?" intervened Centigrade. My own be say those women really try. At least they show say New Maroko jam New Queenstown today. They show say yes something dey for woman body, no be all these girls of nowadays wey dey use their body anyhow. For my abortion clinic, na so them dey rush – like say na chocolate shop. Ah, anyone wey tell you say the world never spoil finish no know anything. But make we leave that talk first. The thing be say our women really try today; they use their body well. The thing wey possess that Segi today na real New Maroko spirit be that. She show them. She show that ASP pepper. See as the man leg dey shake like say earthquake catch am. That Segi na somebody."

"No be say I no like her-o, but I thank God say she no be my daughter."

"The kin' things wey you dey talk, Idi. You no go pray make your daughter get Segi sense to dey hold herself when she grow up? You no hear wetin Centigrade tell us, *abi* you think say all these girls wey dey naked half and quarter dey show their body for nothing no be people children?"

Idi began to say something, thought better of it and decided to change the subject. "All this our *wahala*, where una think say e go lead to?" he said.

"Na people like Governor Omo-ale na them go answer that one. Maybe one day God go seize them and the whole *wahala* go pass over us."

"Me, like say I get village, time don reach wey person go consider retirement from this Lagos of sorrows."

"No talk like that, Centigrade. Person wey im eyes open no dey enter bush. This Lagos na my final bus stop."

"Thank you, *jare*, Quiet. One day one day person must make am here. Lagos na jackpot capital."

"True, but you no see say na we ordinary people all these muggers-in-power dey use play the jackpot? Even *oyibo* people no wicked us like this. See all these fine His Excellency Avenue and Sir Johnson Street, all na *oyibo* build them! If *oyibo* come back come rule us..."

"*Tufia!*" spat Idi.

"Na only person wey no know im ancestry na im fit talk like that."

A livid Centigrade came to an abrupt halt and sized Quiet up. Idi stepped between the two. "Which kin' stupid talk be that?" he said to Quiet.

"I sorry well well," Quiet responded. "Sometimes sef na so my mouth dey foolish."

"Of course, we know," said the peacemaker. "That's why you shout 'Quiet!' for silent church."

With Centigrade pacified, the men walked on.

The crowd was by this time winding its way homeward through the narrow streets of the area of Greater Lagos known as Brazilian Quarters. The narrow streets had clearly not anticipated the upsurge in human and vehicular traffic caused by the transformation of the environs into the country's foremost business district. Some of the earlier settlers were returnees from Brazil, and they had built houses modeled after the ones they had known in Bahia and other such places. Although the population had since become quite mixed and many more houses that owed nothing to Brazilian architecture had sprung up, the original edifices still predominated. There was a carnivalesque atmosphere in the Quarters that was the liveliest celebration of Christmas the marchers had seen so far. The spectacle so overwhelmed Haile, who was marching in the front row with Shanka, Prinzi, and Razaki, that he sang spontaneously:

   O Maroko
   Christmas e don come-o

When you go do your own?
Don't you know it's Christmas time?
Don't you know it's Christmas time?

Prinzi looked at him with a frown. "What was that? Certainly the most unmusical composition I've ever heard. My ears are still tingling with shock."

"Little tingles, I'm sure. What then will Prinzi be without extravaganza?" Haile retorted.

"Actually, it wasn't a bad song," said Shanka. "Except for the pessimism."

"A song is not a sermon, *Mr* Shanka."

It was Shanka's turn to frown at Prinzi.

"I wish Alhaja Maraki were here today," said Razaki. "That woman has quite a sense of drama. When she wants, she can be more Brazilian than Brazilian Quarters."

"She may have taken refuge in one of these houses for all we know."

"Oh no," said Shanka. "I understand she's gone to Europe to visit her daughters."

"You appear to have become an authority on all matters," Prinzi remarked.

"Authority speaking," Shanka said with a shrug.

"Is that the phase before Authority Stealing?"

"Prinzi!" exclaimed Haile. "Don't mind him, Shanka."

"What's going on here?" asked Prinzi. "I notice that Haile speaks for Shanka but that Shanka does not speak for Haile."

"I and I is one."

"This Rastafarian act cost you dearly before the Relocation Board, Haile. Do you want it to cost you your head before you give it up? My friend, Shanka and Haile aren't one. You're an aspiring musician, so you should have an ear for sound. Does 'Shankaile' have the same sound as 'Shankaita'?"

"I see you've found a new game, Pincer," Haile said almost without opening his mouth and walked away.

"Pincer?" Razaki said in between fits of laughter.

"You're being very unfair to Alhaji Kaita," Shanka said to Prinzi. "I assure you that he's the best thing that has ever happened to Maroko. He is indeed venerable."

"He must be godlike then."

Shanka looked at him searchingly, then he moved away in the same direction as Haile.

"That you resent Shanka, the new Shanka, is obvious," Razaki said to Prinzi. "But the smart thing may not be to keep calling his attention to the fact."

"The fellow just rubs me the wrong way. I strongly believe that he and Kaita are up to no good."

"The world is a stage, Prinzi, and the backstage moves to the front stage at the appointed time."

"Whose time? If the time is of their choosing, so too will be the revelation. While we're still pondering the transformation of Shanka, in steps Alhaji Kaita – in the guise of the Jesus of New Maroko. With Shanka at the center, or quite close, whatever it is must be grimy and dangerous."

"To see the great Prinzi reduced to abject wonderment, what a pity. Well, I'll tell you what it's all about."

"You know?" Prinzi asked with surprise.

"It's really simple. All the intrigues in this world usually have one main goal: power. Even if I don't noise it about, unlike you, I have been working on a play, *Behind the Mask*. It begins with a confession by a character not much unlike Kaita to the effect that he has discovered that it is not money that gives happiness in this world but power."

Prinzi hissed. "You, Razaki! You're generalizing the particular when the situation calls for particularizing the general. As for your one-line play-mask, accept my sympathy but certainly no kinship. After people have been celebrated for writing plays without any words at all, I'm amazed you can't get a better deal for yourself with one whole sentence."

"I should have known the twists you're capable of. You're really cut out for talking, not writing. You should start some sort of

Speakers' Corner in New Maroko."

"Well, let them build the Anniversary Square first."

"What devilry are you planning this time?"

"Simple. Theirs is to do the building, ours the conversion. Talking about power, I think we witnessed an interesting kind today. What the women did back there was a dance of power. Maroko was clearly the victim of a plot to separate the scum from the cream – in the government's view. Power is very class-conscious. New Maroko is about to become the victim of another plot. Power is such a ravenous cannibal. Back there, confronted with the disruptive power of New Queenstown and the police, the women chose another vehicle of power. Segi's act was the affective dance within a dance, not too common. When power confronts power, there is often a stalemate."

"Until the greater power wins."

"And the cycle begins again. But that Segi is a fantastic dancer, I must say. Maybe I'll begin the section on Maroko in my novel with her dance at the Bonus Club."

"Why not with Haile and his 'White Christmas'?"

"Not a bad idea from a one-sentence playwright. Haile has become a pawn. The pity is that power exorcises its karma, or strives to, by sacrificing its pawns. For a BA History Attempted, Haile is such a poor Rastafarian. Hey, what's going on here?"

The crowd had finally turned its last street corner before New Maroko. It was the sight of the settlement that had caused the marchers to surge forward. As the crowd approached New Maroko, Shanka called a halt.

"My people," he said. "Welcome back to New Maroko. Although we were stopped from fulfilling our mission in their so-called New Queenstown, our spirit has vindicated us. Let each person now light his candle. We will hold the vigil at the proposed site for the Anniversary Square."

With Shanka at the front, the candlelit procession moved toward the Bonus Club, to the place where Alhaji Kaita had promised to build an Anniversary Square.

As the crowd began to settle down at the site in front of the Bonus Club, a strange thing happened. A cavalcade of white cows appeared at the other end of the road and began walking majestically toward the crowd. All the cows were garlanded and had red dots on their foreheads. Each one carried around its neck a colorful Christmas card. At a sign from Shanka, the cows halted. Moving from cow to cow, he removed the cards. Each bore the sentence: "To the people of New Maroko: Greetings of the season." Each was signed in the same manner: "K-a-a-b-i-y-e-s-i!"

"My people, instead of the one cow we would have slaughtered in honor of the Hump, we now have ten," Shanka said to the puzzled assembly. "Let us slaughter some for a barbecue tonight and share the rest at dawn for our Christmas meals."

The cows were led away by volunteer cooks.

"Who is Kaabiyesi?" The question was a collective quest for comprehension.

"At last, Kaabiyesi," said Shanka. "My people, Kaabiyesi is our great benefactor. He lives on Crocodile Island, which henceforth he wishes to be known as Kaabiyesi Island. Alhaji Kaita and I are his agents, and we all are his tenants."

"Which day this one start again?" someone wondered.

"Kaabiyesi makes himself known only at the appropriate time. He enjoys living alone on the island, tending his pet crocodiles and working on his farm, where he grows all his needs."

"Come on, Shanka," said Prinzi. "How did this Kaabiyesi of yours get to the island? I mean, who is he and where is he from?"

"Kaabiyesi is the Prince of the Atlantic. He is the spirit of the Atlantic made flesh and he has chosen the people of New Maroko as his people. He will stay for a hundred years on earth, and this will be the Age of New Maroko when a people once rejected will dazzle the world. You see, Kaabiyesi is Beauty Incarnate."

"Em, *Mr* Shanka," said Ashikodi, "since you know so much about *Mr* Kaabiyesi, perhaps you can tell us whether he has a tail or a fin. Most things from the river do."

"Of course, Kaabiyesi does have a tail," Shanka responded with an equally mischievous glint in his eyes. "New Maroko is Kaabiyesi's tail."

Another manifestation came then in the form of a garlanded white horse, which came galloping toward the crowd from the same direction as the nine cows. It stopped in front of Shanka – without any gesture from him this time. On its forehead was also a single red dot. Shanka amazed the assembly by prostrating before the white horse as if before an unseen rider. "K-a-a-b-i-y-e-s-i!" he cried.

Before the incredible eyes of people like Razaki, Ashikodi, Prinzi, Segi, who remained on their feet, many people followed the example of Shanka.

"What then will power be without its spectacles?" Prinzi said.

Shanka got up and led the horse back the way it had come. Silence preceded him. Silence followed him.

When the assembly finally settled down to the vigil, the people pondered both the idea of Kaabiyesi and the confrontation at New Queenstown – before dwelling on Maroko, its death throes. In this manner, on that eventful Christmas Eve, New Maroko remembered Maroko.

Book 2
Maroko

Five

The Bonus Club was the heartbeat of Maroko. Although it was an elementary building, many Maroko residents considered it the center of social life – with Segilola as its epicenter. That night, the loudspeakers were playing fast-paced highlife music when she appeared. Clad in a transparent, navel-showing blouse and a skimpy, pleated skirt with hair beads and anklets for effect, she looked ravishing.

Her dance was an acrobatic invocation, and it usually had her mostly male audience crying for more. Her sinuous grace as a dancer heightened the appeal of a song about a young woman who rejects the ways of her village and runs to the city in search of fabled dazzles. In battling with the harsh reality that confronts her, however, she becomes a village fable *sans* dazzle. With the singer detailing the libidinous ways of city men, Segi shrugged off her blouse and skirt with practiced charm, revealing satin underwear. In the ensuing din, her audience showered her with money and love notes.

Extending her dance routine, she began a fetching demonstration of the rhythm of sexual intimacy. Some of the men understood then that, that night, she was giving them a treat to lighten the season of gloom that had begun for them that day. Her legend grew. As she ended her dance with an upward thrust, a "wave of Bonus Club madness" – as Ashikodi was wont to describe the effect – possessed her audience.

Back in her upper floor bedroom overlooking the street, Segi turned on the ceiling fan and cleaned off the rivulets of sweat coursing down her body. She then switched off the light and sat in front of the window – something she often did after her performance downstairs. From this vantage point, she could see all of Maroko – the rusty zinc and the thatched roofs held down with stones and all sorts of rudimentary anchors; the wide veranda of Alhaji Osunwunmi's house, the tallest in the neighborhood; the winking lights of the Green Parrot Hotel; the deserted marketplace adjacent to the motor park, with Mama Badejo's kiosk in the foreground; the forested hill; the stilted huts by the lagoon – including the Church of Maroko beside a rickety school; and the stamp of poverty and squalor almost everywhere.

She was still in front of the window meditating on the sights and sounds of Maroko at night when the men began to pour out from the Bonus Club into the streets and then onward to their respective destinations. She knew all of them, sometimes right down to their first visit to the club.

"Why don't you take in a man or two, at least?" Madam Bonus had once asked her. "You're a woman, you know."

"I have promised myself not to simply become a sex commodity. Sometimes, outside, it's different. I follow my heart."

"So, why do you dance the way you do? Not that I am complaining. In my time at the Shrine, I was even naughtier."

"I dance for the Bonus Club and for Maroko. But, really, when I'm on the dance floor, I simply surrender to the rhythm. I'm only trying to make the best of a life that could be better."

"Always, life can – should, really – be better."

"You should have been a philosopher, madam."

"Look at you! Why do you think I drink so much?"

As the men exited the club, she divided them according to a color chart in her mind – shades of blue for those she sometimes silently dedicated her dance to and shades of red for others. Ashikodi was the last to come out – a bright blue. He lit a cigarette and began to address the unlit window.

"Even though my eyes disappoint me as always, my mind fails me not, Segilola. You are the elusive song that haunts me, the balm of sunlight for every pain. And I will always sing your praise names. Listen to me, Segilola, you with the name that sounds like the lull of deep rivers: distant whispers are not lost on the ears of the wind. And I am the son of the wind. Someday..."

Segi was moved anew and, as the man began to depart, she threw a cork at him. He ran after it, picked it up as if it were a gold coin, then projected his voice until it was a whisper in her ear: "Someday..."

"Listen to me, Maroko, you that never sleep. I dedicate this night and the day after to Segilola," he bawled from the street as if he owned the hours after midnight, cast his cigarette into a gutter and went away whistling "Segi the Lola," a characteristic composition of his.

Segi's soft laughter floated after him before she went to take her bath. He did not hear it, but he believed he did. He walked toward the motor park, hailed Idi and some other men smoking marijuana beside Mama Badejo's kiosk and continued on his way still whistling "Segi the Lola."

"This Ashikodi sef na wa-a," said Idi. "Where e dey go by this kin' time?"

"I hear say na Coconut Island im dey live, but person wey no know go think say im be Maroko person."

"*Abi* na Bonus Club person? That Segi don spoil im head finish."

"Your own *nko*?"

"My brother, that Segi na real temptation-o! You see the kin' dance wey she do tonight? Na so my member just stand like say e wan craze."

"No let Ashikodi hear you-o. E go use dictionary swear for you."

"Which Ashikodi? You think say Segi go 'gree for person like Ashikodi wey im head no correct?"

"Ah, him head correct too much; that na im be im problem. That's why person like am wey dey speak English pass Pastor David dey live the kin' life-without-compass wey we dey see. You no see say na book people like Razaki and Prinzi and Haile na them be im friends?"

"Segi! Segi! Segi! How everybody wan' craze sef because of one *ashawo*?" Shanka wondered.

All the others crowded threateningly around the offender. "Look, if you call her *ashawo* again, we go break your head take your brain do pepper soup. How she be *ashawo*? Because she dey dance so-tey the music dey get flesh and blood? You think say Segi be like that your *ashawo* girlfriend, Epi, for Green Parrot wey be your bank account?"

"Make una no kill me for nothing. I just dey play."

"Shanka Baba! That no be better play-o."

"Leave that one first. Trouble dey town!"

"Say all of us must comot for Maroko? God dey."

"Abeg, make we see road. If you wan' learn pastor work, make you go meet that *wayo* Pastor David. Which one be say 'God dey' for inside?"

The previous day, the state government had issued an order asking Maroko residents to relocate within seven days. Most of the residents were squatters, and the order had cited that fact. All certified or legal occupants were to be temporarily resettled. The news had sent a chill down the spine of Maroko.

"Them say the ocean don nearly chop Maroko finish for under ground; if we no comot quick, the whole place go sink bury all of us."

"Na so world be? All these authority-stealing government people wan' make the world believe say they care about us when their thief thief government don bury us inside suffering finish."

"Na so the world be. If we die finish, who go come dey serve them dey make them feel say na them get the world? Na there rich man care for poor man finish, no be anything else."

"Na wa-o," chipped in a gangly man who had been napping but who now stood up and began to roll a generous quantity of marijuana.

"Quiet!" the men shouted as they acknowledged his awakening. "Quiet in church!"

In the Church of Maroko where the man sometimes served as a warden, he had earned the name by shrilling the order – upon awakening from an untimely nap – in the silence occasioned by Pastor David's sermon. Almost no one called him by any other name after that day.

"You *nko*, Shanka, wey dey pump baby grasscutter until e go big like goat before you sell am?" the man protested. "Anyone dey call you Rabbit or Pump?"

Shanka lashed out, but Idi blocked his advance and managed to draw him away.

"Why your head dey hot like this, Shanka, *abi* them don swear for you for inside bush?" he said. "Na this kin' thing na im dey make poor men kill themselves like fowl. How many times you don see big men dey fight themselves like two cocks wey them inject for brain? But if them wan' deal with poor man na still another common man na im them go manage give cigarette money send go. Make we dey help ourselves."

"Idi Baba!" hailed the other men. "Sometimes sef you fit talk pass Pastor David."

"Like say you go school you for even talk pass Prinzi sef."

"Make una settle proper," Idi invited the two men, "make we dey 'tory dey go. I dey off tomorrow, so I fit take this night make omelet."

Cheered by their colleagues, Shanka and Quiet shook hands.

"Na so life suppose be," said Idi. "No gain inside *wahala*. But come-o, how we wan' do this thing? Where man wan' go for this Lagos wey 'e remain small make people dey waka on top of other people?"

"That na one *wahala*. The other one be say how life wan' be when we scatter finish? Life go lose its color no be small. No Ashikodi, no Prinzi, no Shanka, no Quiet, no Bonus Club, no Segi, no Green Parrot sef, even Pastor David. Ah, that one no go be life again."

"Idi, na you dey talk like this? Life no dey finish. Na inside Maroko you wan' die before?"

"Ah, sometimes life dey finish-o, Shanka, man go come dey chop leftover think say na im original food be that."

"But this government too wicked. Na how many landlords dey for Maroko wey them wan' resettle? So, make all of us jump enter Atlantic Ocean? In short, we no dey go."

Without any other prompting, they began to chant: "We no dey go-o, we no dey go; from Maroko, we no dey comot."

The same chant was taken up, differently, at the Bonus Club later that morning. Madam Bonus had summoned all the girls and other workers to her first-floor suite just before midday. Except for Segi and Linda, the club manager and the head girl respectively, who sat beside her on the bed, and the bartender, Ray, who sat on an armchair, all the others sat on the rug. The short, middle-aged bartender had a knife scar across his face and had been so nicknamed because of his penchant for seeing "a ray of hope" in every circumstance.

"My darlings," began Madam Bonus, "you must have heard of the new trouble in town. What are we going to do?"

"Ah, madam," said a prettified Linda, "you dey always tell us say life na motion."

"It's a line from a song that was popular in my time," the woman said, a nostalgic look flitting across her face as she lit a slim cigarette and passed the pack around. "Well, if they pull Maroko down, we must move on to another place – at least until they finish the renovation or whatever. But we should remain together."

The girls expressed their agreement.

"I think we should move with Maroko," said Segi. "I can't imagine a Maroko without a Bonus Club or a Bonus Club without Maroko.

"Are you afraid you'll lose all your secret lovers?" Madam Bonus said jovially, causing a ripple of laughter.

"Ashikodi, especially," said Ray. "Maybe we should consider moving to Coconut Island. My only fear is that the man might die of excessive joy."

"You think so?" asked Joy, who was so called because of her simulated orgasms.

"True, Maroko men go die finish if they no fit see Segi's the-more-you-look-the-more-you-see dance. E don reach when some of them dey call her name when they dey with us."

"Charity!" screamed Segi in mock rage.

"All right, all right," cut in Madam Bonus, clapping her hands. "Let's get serious."

"I think there's still a ray of hope..." began the bartender.

"Up Ray!" shouted the girls in unison.

"Hip! Hip! Hip!"

"Ray!"

"Seriously, I see a ra...oh, what I mean is that this is not the first time there's been talk about demolishing Maroko..."

"But this time around," said Madam Bonus, "the government is in earnest. All my contacts – policemen, soldiers, civil servants – have confirmed this to me. Five more days to go and the Maroko we know will cease to exist."

"Eh?" Everyone sat up as if rudely awakened. They all knew how much a place like the Bonus Club depended on such contacts to stay in business and how Madam Bonus worked hard to ensure their reliability.

"What are we going to do, madam?"

"I think we should continue on the road that Mama Segi and I carefully chose when we decided to set up the Bonus Club." All the girls understood the reference to how the two women had set up the club, in Maroko, both as a business and as a social service. They had decided to keep only a few girls at a time. To prepare for retirement, each girl had to contribute a part of her earnings into a retirement fund held in trust for her and to learn a trade.

"I don't think that Maroko will disappear entirely, especially with the planned resettlement of 'certified occupants.' As a landlord, I should get a place in this new Maroko and it would be business as usual, more or less."

Ray led the chant this time. "Hip! Hip! Hip!"

"Bonus!"

"Now, Ray, a drink for all of us before I die of a strong thirst."

The ray and the bonus were somewhat reenacted later in

the day at Prinzi's Café. A snack bar, the place was the favorite rendezvous for the "intellectual aristocrats" of Maroko, Prinzi's favorite description, and their associates from outside the settlement.

That evening, the focus of the conversation was on the eviction notice. The bar was almost empty except for Razaki, Ashikodi, Haile, who had popped in from his adjoining record shop for a "quickie" – his term for a quick drink – and Maina, a journalist. From Haile's shop, Fela's "Unknown Soldier" filled the air.

"You're becoming a sadist, Haile," remarked Razaki. Everyone is crying about the eviction notice and you're playing 'Unknown Soldier' – a song about the so-called unknown soldiers who destroyed Kalakuta Republic."

"That is philosophy, brother. The music is saying to Maroko: I and I is one. They destroyed Kalakuta; it rose again. They are about to destroy Maroko; it will rise again. I and I is one. Is that sadism?"

"You're becoming as bad as Prinzi. I used to know a lawyer called Lawyer Ikpeama: The Counsel Who Never Loses. Even when he did, which was not infrequent, he would point out to his clients the importance of not overrating temporary setbacks."

"Maroko needs such a lawyer now," said Maina.

"Why?"

"Because it doesn't have a case that will impress any regular judge. The land in question is the ancestral land of the Marakis. But all land rights are ultimately vested in the government, according to its own decree. And the government has decided to redevelop the land. Case closed."

"Is that all?"

"There's a vague clause about compensation in the land decree. And there have been vague talks about compensation. What else?"

"Plenty. Maroko is old, older than Segi..."

"World people!" exclaimed Ashikodi. "Must you drag her name into this?"

"OK, Maroko is more than twenty years old. Did the government discover its own law only the day before yesterday? Where has its urban planners been all these years?"

"Let's say I have a bad tooth. Do you think it'll be good medical advice for a dentist to tell me: 'Your tooth has been rotting for years, so let it rot'?"

"This sort of analogy can only be uttered in such a place as Prinzi's Café."

"I smell slander," cautioned Prinzi. "If you don't watch out, you'll be hearing from Lawyer Ikpeama soon. But, seriously, people are people. Why must Maroko be demolished within one week? Maroko can possibly be resettled to everyone's benefit with more thoughtfulness than is the case at present."

"But you have to consider the circumstances. Maroko is sinking..."

"Someone has been reading about Atlantis upside down. The same government that has never cared about people living almost in a cesspool is now brimming with antiseptic phrases of salvation. It's cheap propaganda, and it shows that these people, even in their decadence, know that what they're about to do is evil. Let me tell you, it's a ruse to expand Queenstown. The only reclamation that needs to be done is to clean up that Shit Lagoon."

"I never knew that we had a clairvoyant among us."

"There are many things you don't know. In this country, the future is an open book for those who can read."

"What a barkeeper you are, castigating your customers while they're putting food on your table!"

"In case you haven't noticed, there's an invisible sign at the entrance that clearly states: 'Right of Entry Reserved.' Prinzi's Café is a privilege."

"That's the problem we have in this country – citing invisible signs."

"Thou shalt not covet thy neighbor's property," quoted Ashikodi.

"Ah, a Jehovah among us too!"

"Gentlemen," cut in Haile before Ashikodi could respond. "We're deflecting the subject. Even the government is not clapping for itself, so why is Maroko taking the news calmly?"

"There will be reactions after the shock has sunk in. I don't know about you, but I'm here because Maroko is a microcosm of this country. In your Rastafarian culture, I know there's a 'soon come' attitude of waiting philosophically for God's own time, although you don't seem to be a good example. In Nigeria, there is a 'soon arrive' syndrome – the certainty by everyone on the streets that they will soon 'make it' even within this system, so no one wants to seriously rock the system but to ride each storm instead. So, we keep moving from cesspool to cesspool. Ah, I could use that in my novel, you know."

"Must you be so tiresome?"

"But what's the big deal about relocating Maroko?" Maina asked. "The place is a den of thieves and touts. Why is everyone talking as if it's some sort of paradise or oasis rather than a festering slum in need of liberation?"

"Maroko is a refuge for the poor. And the poor, like any other class, has its own litany of the good and the bad. Many here cannot afford to live anywhere else – not in Greater Lagos or Queenstown, certainly. And that is why they're scared to leave. Many have nowhere else to go – except perhaps under flyovers or on the streets of another slum. Sounds worse than a familiar slum."

"Talk, talk, talk!" protested Haile. "We should be organizing a reaction, a deafening shout across the wall."

"What sort of reaction do you propose, Haile? Do you think that the people are incapable of carving their own resistance masks? Look at what happened in Bakalori. A village of farmers and fishermen stood up, although unsuccessfully in the end, against a government plot to dam the natural flooding that was their vital life support system."

"I trust you to cite a thousand instances if need be. But this is the time for action, Prinzi."

"I'm a writer, my friend."

"Why have you never said: 'I'm a writer, not an entrepreneur'?"

"Being a writer doesn't particularly qualify anyone to lead a street march, unless he is also streetwise and brave."

"Are you such a coward, Prinzi?"

"My friend, we all have the capacity for bravery. All we have to do is discover it. But bravery isn't my desired contribution to civilization. I have set my chest against the literary masters instead. However, if you think I'm going to let the mindless uprooting of Maroko happen just like that, you don't even know Prinzi."

"So, what are we going to do?"

"We should pool together our abilities. But please note that to stand in front of a moving tank is not bravery – unless the tank halts."

"But how will it halt if you don't stand in its way?"

"That's the point. You have to understand the monsters you're dealing with and strategize."

The eviction notice was also the subject of the sermon preached by Pastor David the next day at the Church of Maroko. A dapper fellow with a well-groomed beard who unmistakably loved his immaculate suits, leather shoes, and a rose in his buttonhole, the pastor was renowned for his histrionics. Dubbed "Pastorator" by Prinzi, his church was a stilted hut beside the lagoon. But it was the Sunday event for the residents of the Green Parrot Hotel, the Bonus Club, and many others in Maroko since swept off their feet by the man's flourishes and promises of miracles. Inside, several ceiling fans and bowls of incense battled, sometimes successfully, the stench from the lagoon – measures the pastor said he had initiated to calm his more vocal critics who had begun to refer to the church as "the Shit Church" or "the Shit of Maroko." When he set up the church, the area was about the only available space in the overcrowded settlement. He had responded to the initial reluctance of many residents to attend a church there with the explanation that he chose the location and the stilts to illustrate that salvation and the levitation of the spirit knew neither boundaries nor adversity. The explanation was quickly followed by extravagant promises. According to him, the Holy Spirit had placed him in charge of riches greater than the national budget, to be distributed to his flock. He would stop in mid-sentence, point to a man or woman and announce a gift of a million naira or an expensive car. The church flourished, drawing many people from outside the settlement, so much so that Pastor David began to talk of moving to "a permanent site."

That Sunday, the third day after the eviction notice, his reading was one of his favorites, a passage from Corinthians.

"*If I speak with the tongues of men, and of angels, and have not charity, I am become as sounding brass or tinkling cymbal. And if I should have prophecy and should know all mysteries and all knowledge, and if I should have all faith, so that I could remove mountains, and have not charity, I am nothing. And if I should distribute all my goods to feed the poor, and if I should deliver my body to be burned, and have not charity, it profiteth me nothing. Charity is patience, is kind; charity envieth not, dealeth not perversely, is not puffed up. Is not ambitious, seeketh not her own, is not provoked to anger, thinketh no evil; rejoiceth not in iniquity, but rejoiceth with the truth; beareth all things, believeth all things, hopeth all things, endureth all things.*"

"I have heard the cries of Maroko," he told his congregation with his familiar fervor. "My God has heard them too. And the Lord is good. Someone please say 'Hallelujah!' There is no doubt that those seeking to destroy Maroko lack charity. They have not learned patience, kindness, and compassion. No doubt, the Lord will deal with them according to their deeds. I tell you, today, people of Maroko: the perpetrators of iniquity shall not go unpunished."

A yell of assent rose from the bowels of the church, amid which could be discerned such phrases as "O yes!," "Yes, pastor!," "O yes, Lord!" Quiet managed to restrain himself from calling for quietude, but he paused in his routine of rousing those inclined to nap even during such a dramatic 'vaganza as Pastor David's sermon.

"In the face of such iniquity, however, Maroko must still bear all things, believe all things, hope all things, endure all things. Thousands of years ago, the Son of God taught us the eternal Christian lesson of turning the other cheek. The meek, we are told, shall inherit the earth. We are people of the spirit, not land-grabbers; children of light, not darkness. And I tell you, today, the heart of Maroko, which appears – only an appearance, mind you – almost yanked out will beat again. The Great Lord sleepeth not. Beware of this hour of temptation that it does not drive you into iniquity. Temptation shall come, and it has, but woe to the person through whom temptation comes; greater woe even to the person who falls to temptation. We are people of God, and the Lord has already won the battle. His banner over us is love. We have His promise on that. And God is not a man that He should lie.

"In the midst of bad news, the Holy Spirit has asked me to announce tidings of great joy. To every person present here in this church today, He has asked me to give one million naira as resettlement grant..."

The ensuing tumult was so thunderous that Quiet reflexively bellowed "Quiet! Quiet in church" – a whimper in a gale – before he joined in the applause, the backslapping, embraces, and other forms of celebration.

A smiling Pastor David wiped sweat off his face with an exquisite handkerchief and made a sign to Quiet and his co-workers to immediately initiate the offertory procession. Right on cue, the choir struck up a song:

> He has made me proud
> He has made me proud
> I will rejoice and praise His name
> For He has made me proud
> P-r-o-u-d!

Six

To many in Maroko, the house was known as Maraki Palace, although its owner had named it Faith Villa. A mansion reminiscent of the Brazilian baroque period, it was the best house in the slum. The few people who had been inside told tales of leather armchairs, damask curtains, haughty servants, and robust pets – some in colorful cages. The parrot, which was said to chant "Madam, abeg" at some callers, a reflection of the nature of their visit, was the most notorious.

Alhaja Osunwunmi, the owner, was a frail, often overdressed woman known for her unpredictable headgears and rimless glasses. Because she was hardly ever seen on the streets except as an occasional, backseat blur being chauffeured out of or into the settlement, her presence in the slum sometimes provoked arguments and revelations.

"I see that una Pastor David dey go inside Maraki Palace yesterday," Epi told some of her colleagues at the Green Parrot Hotel one evening. Her bright, rolling eyes had earned her the nickname "Epi Eye."

"Which one be 'that una Pastor David'? Talk true, Epi Eye, if the man give you money, you no go sleep with am?"

"Which kin' question be that? *Ashawo* na short-time contract, *abi* your own different? But that kin' man no go come Green Parrot when plenty women for im church don nearly craze because of am. And I hear say e rich well well. But wetin be im own with Osunwunmi? The woman na Muslim, the man na pastor."

"As Maroko small reach, I never take my eye see that alhaja. Una sure say she no be story?"

"Me, I don hear her voice reach two times, when I sneak into her house go sleep with Goomsi."

"Goomsi no be houseboy? E no fit come sleep with you here?"

"Hmm, Goomsi no be ordinary houseboy-o. The kin'

money wey e dey give me pass houseboy matter."

"Queen, Queen! Me, I don see the alhaja once. She no be story at all."

"You take your eyes see am?"

"Na wetin I for use before?"

"Her children, *nko*? You don see them too?"

"They say the two wey she get dey abroad. Ah, I dey go work-o. See that Ignatius as e dey wink at me like say e wan' craze."

"Ah, *ashawo* no easy-o."

"You think say Maroko na Portuguese Quarters before? But, at least, Ignatius sabi grammar small, although no be that one person go chop."

"Maybe that im wonder friend Ashikodi..."

"That one, I never see am here pass two, three times."

"How e go come here? Segi don spoil im head."

The next morning, the day after Pastor David's sermon on charity, Alhaja Osunwunmi opened a new chapter in her legend. At midday, her *mai guard* walked into the street in front of the house, bent his head toward the east, cupped his hand around his ear and began the longest call to prayer anyone in Maroko had ever heard.

Allaaaaaaahhuuuuuuuh Akbar!
Allaaaaaaaaaaaaaahhuuuuuuuuuuuuuuuh Akbar!

A crowd assembled almost immediately and stood watching the usually taciturn *mai guard*.

Although Prinzi restrained himself from going as far as the next street where Faith Villa was, the commotion brought him out of his empty bar to Haile's Record Shop. The Rastafarian stood at the entrance, on his toes, peering upwards as if that made observation or comprehension easier.

"Ah, Prinzi himself! It had to take something like this, and an empty bar, to bring you out."

"What's happening?"

"It looks like Jah gonna send down the rain soon."

"Don't even try. You know, anyone could mistake you for

a Rastafarian – until you try to speak the part."

Haile laughed and stood firmly on the ground. "Let's go find out what's happening there."

"Don't be so ordinary. To think is to see – and very clearly, I tell you."

"So, why did you ask?"

"That's the Maroko blood in me. This unusual commotion must have something to do with the eviction notice and the governor's visit today."

"Is the governor coming to Maroko, in this climate of disenchantment?"

"You play this Shrine music all day and all night, so much so that you don't know anything else."

"But what can this have to do with the visit of that land thief, Omo-ale?" wondered Haile. "Either that recluse has finally gone mad because of too much solitude and living in the past or this is a sure sign of the end time."

"You believe in that?"

"Sure. When Selassie, the Lion of Judah, returns."

"You Rastafarian fraud! Sing that to your expatriate dupes hunting for the soul of Africa in readymade stores. Hey, I could use that, you know."

"In an invisible corner of an invisible novel? Not a bad idea. Anyway, it says in the Bible that many strange and crazy things will happen during the End Time. Like this call to prayer at the wrong hour. Like that dandy, Pastor David..."

"I'm yet to recover from that shock. In walks an obvious fraud like Pastor David, builds a church on top of centuries of shit, yet he has a congregation going in no time. And the more he rips the people off, the greater their devotion."

"It's the 'soon arrive' syndrome, the sort that says: 'One day, soon, my ship will arrive and I'll be at the airport.'"

"It's getting curiouser and curiouser, that's for sure. The great Maroko novel is practically writing itself."

Allaaaaaaahhuuuuuuuuh Akbar!

Allaaaaaaaaaaaaaahhuuuuuuuuuuuuuuh Akbar!

In a secluded part of her mansion, Alhaja Osunwunmi, dressed in a white gown and a feather headband, stood in her personal Shrine of Greatness. The very few people who knew her well knew that she was steeped in her genealogy. To such people, she would often speak about her ancestors – including the one who was a counselor in the court of a Brazilian king, the one who fought as one of Ashipa's commanders in the War of Dahomey, and the one who could trace his descent right up to Oduduwa. With such people, she would discuss how fate had robbed her of her husband and her people of their vast lands – except for Maroko. Although Maroko teemed with the wretched of the earth, it was the last pointer to her ancestors' greatness and she was the last link in a long human chain, except for two daughters who had settled down in Europe. In her crying solitude, she wept often over her fate – inside a shrine in which statues of her more outstanding ancestors stood around a bowl of water in which she sometimes saw the future.

When the government made her an offer for Maroko, she consulted her water bowl and still saw a great future for the Marakis. So, she turned down the offer. When it became obvious to her that the "offer" was actually an order, she began to tearfully invoke her ancestors in the seclusion of her shrine. That morning, she had decided on a combination of methods – a call to the Allah that her grandfather had introduced into the family's religious history and further entreaties to her ancestors before confronting the governor in Maroko.

She did not come out until the call to prayer ceased. It was a signal. In the distance, a siren could be heard wailing its way to Maroko. She quickly reminded Goomsi and her other servants of the proper conduct demanded by such an occasion, then she retired into her bedroom to get ready – a graying annotation in proud parenthesis.

Outside the house, the crowd began to drift toward the marketplace in time to witness the arrival of the military governor's convoy – acrobatic riders, black sedans with tinted glasses, and truckloads of soldiers who looked like harbingers of death. When the convoy came to a halt, and after the soldiers had spilled out of the truck and fanned out, the governor emerged from the most tinted of the sedans. He looked impressive in his plumed beret, the immaculate uniform of a colonel, and a swagger stick. By now, the crowd had become a market of people – including State House correspondents who had come with Governor Raji Omo-ale.

"Fellow Lagosians," the governor addressed the crowd.

A hiss of dissociation answered this form of address – the sort, many people muttered, usually preferred by military rulers.

"I am here today to tell you and to show you that I love you all. I love Maroko. What we are doing is for your own good, for the good of Maroko."

The crowd booed him but not long enough for the gun-toting soldiers to clearly identify the culprits.

"If we don't reclaim this place quickly, the whole of Maroko will sink. We have therefore provided a place to resettle all the residents of Maroko."

An inaudible question reared its head with deafening, gestural insistence.

"Yes, all the residents of Maroko."

Encouraged by the example of some of the governor's aides, the crowd – made up mainly of those who had previously been declared "unresettlable" – began to clap.

Next, the governor called on Alhaja Osunwunmi. Although the crowd followed the convoy through the narrow streets of Maroko smelling like rotting fish and decomposing cadavers, the soldiers barred them from coming near the house. Inside the house, the usual important-sounding nothings common on such occasions were exchanged, the governor accepted several yards of brocade as "the traditional gift of the Marakis to royal and important visitors ever since the War of Dahomey," and the visit was over. Outside, the battery of reporters admitted into the compound but barred from entering the house descended on the alhaja with a barrage of questions.

"I have heard what the governor said," the woman replied to one of them. "I think he was talking sense. But that is only if you look at the matter from the point of view of the government. I think it makes more sense to address the issue with temperance and conscience."

But when Alhaja Osunwunmi watched the news that night, she broke down and wept. The newscaster spoke in clipped tones of the governor's "thoughtful inspection tour" of Maroko, his rapport with the crowd, and his promise to "resettle all the residents of Maroko who are certified occupants." The footage showed the crowd dancing in response and chanting "God is great!" Then there was a clip of the governor's convoy on its way to Faith Villa. According to the newscaster, the governor and the alhaja "held frank discussions" behind closed doors. The subsequent footage showed Alhaja Osunwunmi telling State House Correspondents: "I have heard what the governor said. I think he was talking sense." End of story.

Many people in Maroko did not watch the newscast, but they woke up to a six-inch headline in the government newspaper: "Maroko Agrees to Move – Legal Residents to Be Resettled, Landowner Backs Government." They began to congregate in front of the Maraki Palace in various degrees of rage. Razaki and Prinzi arrived with armloads of placards denouncing the government for its propaganda and land-grabbing propensity. Razaki had heard the newscast in his "boys quarters" at Tarzan Jetty; he had put on his clothes and rushed down to Prinzi's Café. He met almost a full house – Prinzi, Ashikodi, and several others.

"Hey, fellows, have you heard the news?"

"I haven't," said Prinzi, "but I can tell its chemical property just by looking at you."

"The barkeeper speaks of chemical property," muttered Ashikodi.

"I hope you're not contemplating slander, or else you'll ruin your credit here," cautioned Prinzi.

"The intellectual as a dictator."

"A fitting title for a Prinzian non-book, I believe," said Razaki. "But you people aren't listening to me. It's just been announced on television that Maroko has made a deal with Governor Omo-ale to move within four days and that only legal occupants will be resettled. Is that true?"

"The man is just being Governor Colonel Omo-ale," Prinzi said.

"What about the bit about Alhaja Osunwunmi speaking in support of the government?"

"I don't know what transpired between the two, but I've met the woman twice and she doesn't strike me as someone who will support the government's bid to rob her of her ancestral land. In any case, the bloody government is made up of politicians reared in an Academy of Lies and Aggrandizement."

"So, what happens now?"

"The intellectual man of action."

"Cut it out, Ashikodi. I think the time has come for a protest march. I'll craft the placards – they should be crafted, you know, to be worthy of its writer – and get Haile when he comes back from the Shrine to provide a recording device and a public address system. You Razaki should be able to creatively utilize the people of Maroko for a communal theater of agitation. Ashikodi, you're the natural choice to deliver the oration, what with your famous oratory beneath Segi's unlit window."

"This is becoming very interesting, really," Ashikodi said with a smile.

"I'm about to write a novel of protest, man. Not the same thing as a protest novel, you know."

"You will argue behind the leg of a donkey, Prinzi," said Ashikodi and began to ventriloquially sing the national anthem before Prinzi could respond.

That night, the three – excluding Ashikodi, who left with a promise to return early in the morning, but including Haile, who came home at about three o'clock in the morning – applied themselves to their different assignments. By dawn, Razaki had finished his script, Haile had tested the necessary equipment, and Prinzi had produced several placards of rhymed statements. The three then made their way to Faith Villa.

"My friends," Prinzi addressed the restive crowd, while Haile and Razaki distributed the placards, "sheathe your daggers and listen to the voice of reason. Alhaja Maraki-Osunwunmi is one of us, and I believe she was misrepresented. Maina, the author of that report in *The Echo*, happens to be an acquaintance of mine – I have all sorts, you know. Maina as a State House correspondent in a government newspaper is an apologist who routinely stands the truth on its head. So, we will do the real thing that needs to be done. We will march on the Government House. We will march."

The crowd took up the chant, with some hailing "Prinzi!" "Prinzi for Maroko!"

"And I will march with you," Alhaja Osunwunmi said from her gate.

A low murmur began to swell from the crowd.

"My friends," said Prinzi to the assembly, "let the alhaja speak."

"I will march with you," said the woman once more, as the murmurs subsided. "I will march with you for I have been maligned. It is not an accident that M-a-r-a-k-i, which some people have corrupted to Maroko, is made up of six letters; they represent the six points in the compass of my ancestors..."

The crowd was becoming restive again. Prinzi hurriedly whispered to the heiress.

"We will leave that story for another day," said the woman. "Today, I tell you: Governor Omo-ale is vending a cheap lie. I never came to any agreement with him yesterday. I maintain that he is going about his mission like a conqueror-thief."

The crowd cheered; some chanted "Maraki! Maraki!"

"I have never wavered from the conviction that it is criminal to steal my ancestral heritage with the help of a military edict that says all land belongs to the government and can be taken over for development at a price determined by the government.

Development for whom? I have been made to sign a document that says I am only entitled to the spot where my house stands and a ridiculous sum of money for the rest of Maroko, yet they peddle the lie that I have come to terms with the government. I too have had a study made, and I can tell you that Maroko is not sinking – at least not in the manner being advertised by the government. I have never sold a single piece of Maroko, now the government has taken all of it."

Almost in tears, she had to pause and regain her composure before continuing. "It is true that my husband sold some plots, but I have only made leases. Presently, squatters occupy a large area of the land, as you all know. I must confess that the Marakis do not celebrate poverty, but there is also enough of that in our history and that has made me tolerant. Now, they want to give an apartment for every plot legally bought and a room for every plot legally leased. They claim their New Maroko is of a higher grade in the property market. What about all the squatters to whom Maroko is home? They should jump into the lagoon, I suppose? I, Alhaja Lateefat Awolowo-Maraki-Osunwunmi, I will march with you – the same way my esteemed ancestor marched with Ashipa in the War of Dahomey. We will march together."

The crowd went gaga. Razaki raised the first song in his script, which marked the beginning of the march.

> We will march
> March march to 'ale
> March march for 'roko
> We will march

"My God!" Prinzi exclaimed to Haile. "That woman is a talker."

"I see-e, the homage Cicero pays to Demosthenes. You know that bit, I suppose, about how after Cicero spoke the people said 'How well he spoke,' but after Demosthenes spoke they said 'Let us march.'"

"A little history, plenty of Afrobeat, and a BA Attempted thinks he is Selassie."

"That's in bad taste, Prinzi."

"All right, I'm sorry. But let us march first. You can crack my skull later. Have you seen Ashikodi?"

"How can anyone see the son of the wind?" said Haile lightheartedly, mollified by Prinzi's apology. "But you can be sure he'll make his presence felt at the appropriate time."

The march was in progress. Razaki, now carrying a bedroll on his back and an unlit lantern on his head, and Alhaja Osunwunmi were at the front. From the streets of Maroko, the crowd marched toward His Excellency Avenue in Greater Lagos, the road that led to the Government House. Armed soldiers obstructed the progress of the march. Behind them was a tank, on top of which sat an officer speaking into a walkie-talkie.

"There's too much show of power in this country," Haile said to Prinzi. "Look at this. They must have set this up this morning in anticipation of this march."

"Guns are in power, my friend. What do you expect?"

Razaki called a halt. There was a provision for that in his script. He began a second song:

>   Omo-ale is a goat-o
>   A goat-o
>   Omo-ale is a goat-o
>   B-a-s-t-a-r-d!

Intoxicated by the spirit of the song, the crowd began to surge forward.

"Halt!" commanded the officer on top of the tank as his men pointed their rifles at the crowd.

The motion quickened. The officer then pointed his gun at Razaki and fired. The theater director crumpled on the road. The shock froze the marchers for a moment, then pandemonium seized them – with each person racing back toward Maroko. Prinzi, Haile, and Ashikodi, who had begun to converge around Razaki despite the riotous retreat, were astounded to see the theater director stagger to his feet and join spiritedly in the flight.

The crowd regrouped at the roadside market in Maroko,

but without Alhaja Osunwumni. Shivering and panting, the heiress immediately hurried home. Razaki, it was discovered, had been shot with a rubber bullet. He was declared "the hero of the march." Haile now played back the recording of the march – from Prinzi's address outside the Maraki Palace up until the retreat from His Excellency Avenue. The playback sharpened the mood of the crowd, and Razaki took over once more.

"On behalf of the Maroko Project, we now present to you 'The Governor's Address, Ashikodi's Response,'" he told the crowd. Then he cleared his throat, stood as stiff as a tree and began a hilarious mimicry of the governor's speech the previous day.

"Fellow Lagosians, I am here today to tear you and chew you that I lust you all. I love Myandco. What we are dooming is for your own doom, for the doom of Myandco. If we don't reclaim this prize quickly, Myandco will sink. We have therefore provided a place to resettle all the rats and dents of Myandco."

The crowd applauded.

Ashikodi took the stage. First, he borrowed the pet monkey of one of the residents – a quack doctor known either as Dr Swallow because of his penchant for advising his clients to swallow their saliva as part of their treatment or as Centigrade because he diagnosed almost every ailment with a thermometer. Ashikodi tethered the monkey to an empty stall and Razaki named it Colonel Raji Omo-ale.

"Your Excellency, the Governor of Lagos," Ashikodi said to the monkey. "I know you're only a monkey, and I can see you salivating over the banana that is Maroko. But a banana, your Excellency, isn't always good for a monkey, even one in power. It's been said that we are afraid to move even for our own good. How can that be? Except for the alhaja, no one in this inner city can claim an ancestral bond to the land, yet there are thousands of people here, each a consequence of motion. Every morning, Maroko moves to Greater Lagos, to Queenstown, to power it – as factory hands, security guards, mechanics, and everything else. We are not afraid to move. What you're proposing is not motion; it's erasure. Your Excellency, the Governor of Lagos, you're a monkey, I know, but monkeys have sometimes claimed kinship with humans. May you indeed dream and dare like a human being."

The excited crowd swept Ashikodi off his feet and carried him around the market chanting his praise names. He was named the 'Roko or the Spokesman of Maroko. Omo-ale was labeled the Mar, the Destroyer. From that day onward, no one called Dr Swallow's monkey any other name but Mar.

The soldiers arrived the next day, before dawn, while Maroko was still to fully awaken. Volleys of gunshots fired into the air marked their arrival. Prinzi woke with a start in the backroom of his bar where he slept. The narrow room was furnished with a mattress, heaps of books, and other such Prinzian essentials. Beside him on the mattress, his girlfriend still lay asleep despite the mayhem. He switched on the light and regarded her – a thirtyish, certified caterer with a body that was a work of art. Their relationship was a subject Prinzi rarely discussed with anyone, although he was known to fondly call her "One." Muttering about people who could sleep through Armageddon, Prinzi got up, put on his clothes and tiptoed out of the room. He went to Haile's Record Shop where, he knew, the Rastafarian slept. Despite repeated knocks, however, no sound came from inside.

"Stop playing dead, Haile," he called out.

"I don't know about that," Haile replied drily. "Are you associated in any way with these gunshots?"

"Open the door, man. I'm as mystified as you are."

The door was opened hesitantly. The sight of Haile peeping out from the base of the door made Prinzi hoot with laughter. "Get up, man," he said to the Rastafarian, making a show of raising his hands. "I come in peace."

Haile straightened up and took one step out of the door. "What's going on, man?"

"I wish I knew. Yesterday, we named a monkey Omo-ale and told it off; hours later, this mayhem erupts."

"So, what are we to do?"

"Hang on to life, man. Without that, nothing can be done."

"Sounds to me like everyone wanting to go to heaven but no one wanting to die."

"More like everyone acting tough but no one opening his door with confidence."

A fresh volley of shots sent both Haile and Prinzi scurrying into the dark shop.

Not Shanka. In his one-room residence near the Shit Lagoon, where he and Epi Eye lay in each other's arms that morning, he appeared to be deriving strength from the gunshots.

"You sure say no be that World Bank and im gang handwork be this?" asked Epi Eye.

World Bank was the self-styled sobriquet of an ex-convict resident in Maroko who was commonly believed to be a robber. He was known to sleep through the day and then disappear at night, only to return at dawn. A brute of a man, many people had accepted his nickname because it made him seem less human than Williamson, his baptismal name, did. Shanka was one of his acquaintances.

"No dey call World Bank name anyhow," cautioned Shanka. "The man be like night masquerade-o, but all this *wahala* no be im handwork. E no dey waka bad waka for Maroko."

"Wetin be your own with the man sef?"

"No mind the thing wey people dey talk. Maroko people too talk the thing wey they no know."

"Ah, nothing wey Maroko people no know, na only money them no get. If I tell you half of the things wey I dey see or hear..."

"Time don dey reach when you go comot from that *yeye* Green Parrot where people dey do as they like with you because of toy money."

"Which one be toy money? E be like say you don dey see money, this one wey you dey talk like this," said Epi Eye, putting one leg on top of Shanka.

"Better dey come, that one is sure."

"Eh-he? Your grammar sef be like say e don dey change.

So, na true say one correct car find you come today?"

"Maroko! Person no go fit even piss for im house make the whole Maroko no see am talk."

"You piss inside the car?" asked Epi Eye with a mischievous smile. "Anyway, you wan' hide that one from me, *abi*?"

"*Haba*! I dey plan to surprise you, that's all. Better dey come, Epi Eye. Maroko na R.I.P. be that, but Shanka is born again. Better dey come."

The girl began to massage him stimulatingly. "No forget me-o, Shanka; no forget Epi Eye," she said.

"I can never forget you," said Shanka, responding to the caress.

Another volley of shots, the longest, came once more from the direction of the market.

Madam Bonus could bear it no longer. She unlocked her door and walked to Segi's room, where Linda, Charity, and Ray had already converged.

"Look at you, Ray," she said with mock gravity. "You no dey shame? They're shooting outside and you've come to take refuge in Segi's room."

"That's strategy, madam."

"Are you competing with Ashikodi?"

"Me, I'm a homeboy. I've heard him called a vagabond."

"You *nko*?" snapped Charity. "Once upon a time..."

"Professor of history!" Ray snapped back.

"Cut it out," said Madam Bonus. "I think that Maroko is being invaded. This is the sort of thing that happened in Kalakuta. First, they shot up the peace, then they set upon us like wolves. My God! They threw people down from upstairs windows, raped women, and looted and destroyed everything they set their eyes on. The cruel irony was that their grievous sins conferred on them anonymity. When a soldier commits an atrocity in this country, he becomes an Unknown Soldier. I fear Maroko is about to have its own Unknown Soldier."

"God forbid!"

"I think that someone is out to show Maroko that he's not only in government but in power," said Segi. "Yesterday, I really felt proud of Ashikodi, Razaki, Prinzi, and Maroko. I think that we're now paying the price."

The confirmation came in the form of an announcement made from a vehicle on a tour of the slum: "Good morning, Maroko. This is Captain Emmanuel Doma of the Nigerian Army. This is to inform every resident of Maroko that, following the breach of peace that occurred here yesterday, the Governor of Lagos, His Excellency Colonel Raji Omo-ale, has declared a state of emergency in Maroko with immediate effect. During this period, a curfew will be in effect from six o'clock in the evening until six o'clock in the morning. No congregation of more than two persons, except with prior permission, will be tolerated. All exits from and entrances into Maroko will be monitored. Any attempt to foment unrest will be decisively dealt with. You have been warned."

Captain Doma immediately became known as Captain Doom.

In her Shrine of Greatness, where she had taken refuge, Alhaja Osunwunmi listened to the announcement with a heaving heart. She got up from her kneeling position and walked toward the bowl of water. On its surface, she saw the mausoleum of the Marakis repelling detonating soldiers.

Seven

The exodus began later that morning. Idi was one of the early arrivals at the barricade set up by the soldiers along the exit route. He was on his way to work at Shelling Hotel.

"Halt!" ordered one of the soldiers, pointing a gun at him.

Idi stopped immediately, muttering in his heart: "Which one be this again?"

"Who you be and where you dey go?" barked the soldier.

Idi brought out his identity card, gave it to the soldier and explained that he was going to work.

The man scrutinized the card, then went to consult his superior. Upon his return, he held on to the card and declared: "This ID na fake. We go take you in for questioning."

As the other soldiers began to advance on him, Idi desperately dug out his fare to and from work. The advance stopped.

"Wetin be that?" demanded his interrogator, moving forward and snatching the money. He then flung the ID card at Idi and motioned him forward: "Move!"

Idi picked up his ID card and began the long trek, past the barricade, to the Shelling Hotel, muttering to himself.

Quiet, who came shortly afterward, fared worse.

"Wetin you carry?" the soldier asked him.

"Nothing," he responded rather sheepishly.

Ordered to turn out his pockets, he did so with alacrity, revealing a dirty handkerchief in his shirt pocket and holes in his trouser pockets.

"Who are you, and where you dey go?"

He explained that he was a casual laborer at St Christopher's Bakery in nearby Queenstown and was, as usual, walking to work.

"And your ID?"

Because he was a casual laborer, he explained, he had

none.

"Hmm, where you dey live?"

"For Maroko here, sir."

"Where be 'For Maroko here'? Wetin be the name of the street and the number of the house?"

"I be warden for Church of Maroko, sir. I dey sleep there. Pastor David na my pastor."

"Shut up! You no get proper business here at all. If we find you here again, we go finish you." That sentence pronounced, the soldier ordered him to move – back to Maroko.

Ashikodi heard of these happenings on his way to Maroko. He took a cardboard from a trash can beside the road and wrote on it: "The bearer is new in Maroko. If seen wandering, please direct to Prinzi's Café." With the aid of a string, he hung the notice on his front and continued on his way, whistling 'Segi the Lola.'

At the barricade, the soldiers regarded him with wonder. So directed by their superior, they seized him and "escorted" him to Prinzi's Café. The cardboard notice nearly made Prinzi laugh uproariously, but he managed to restrain himself.

"Are you Prinzi?" demanded one of the soldiers.

"Who can be sure of anything under this circumstance?" said Prinzi.

"You be one of these over-sabi people, eh? Well, do you know this vagrant here?"

"If your Excellency, the honorable sergeant-general, will care to note, I am no vagrant," protested Ashikodi. "Only new in Maroko under the state of emergency."

"What do you mean by 'sergeant-general'?"

"Everyone knows that all soldiers in the Nigerian army are generals – privates, corporals, sergeants, captain-generals. One must bow and tremble before such an army."

"Shut up!" snapped the sergeant. "Search the place!" he ordered the other soldiers.

The search ended in the freezer, with the soldiers taking out three cartons of beer.

"I am confiscating these," the sergeant declared. "And be warned that under the emergency any congregation of more than two people will not be tolerated."

"But this is a bar."

"Congregation is congregation."

With their guns slung over their shoulders and each man carrying a carton of beer, the soldiers took their leave.

"Wonderful!" exclaimed Ashikodi. "Their officer ordered them to bring back Prinzi. They're taking back three cartons of beer instead. It can only happen to a barkeeper, I suppose."

"I think that this calls for a celebration. A beer on the house!"

"Prinzi, how many times will I tell you that one is the number of the devil afflicted with the Great Aloneness?"

"You should know better than try to con me by talking like a Dead Sea scroll. The real devils have just hijacked three cartons of my beer and I didn't observe any Great Aloneness about them. How come they even paid attention to your notice anyway?"

"Welcome to Nigeria," Ashikodi said as he removed the notice.

"You better fetch the drinks while I hang the 'Closed' sign on my door. How can any bar do business if more than two people inside is a contravention of the law?"

They reunited at a table. Prinzi uncorked the drinks.

"When are you moving?" asked Ashikodi.

"Where to?"

"That attitude won't get you anywhere. In Greater Lagos, they're talking about something called the Resettlement Board arriving here today to facilitate the resettlement of all qualified residents."

"Their Resettlement Board is like a mountain. It doesn't move."

"Not this time. They're making a show of actually caring about Maroko residents. A publicity stunt."

"And a dangerous omen. It can only mean that they'll

indeed wipe out Maroko after the deadline."

"Isn't that obvious to you yet? Well, you're welcome to stay with me for as long as you like."

"You know, you're a different man today, Ashikodi. But I think I'll apply for a place in New Maroko. I don't see any future for a barkeeper in a settlement called Coconut Island. People already used to coconut milk aren't likely to appreciate alcohol. Another beer on the house!"

"Viva the accursed emergency!"

Prinzi fetched the drinks.

"I've got a plan," Ashikodi said.

"You, Ashikodi, you've got a what?" Prinzi sat up. "Now I too can say 'Viva the emergency.' You're a different man today, you know."

"You've said that before. And you're wrong. But let's not argue about that. I think we should hold a passage rite tonight. I'll ask Ignatius to construct an effigy of Omo-ale – he sometimes claims to be a canoe-builder, you know – and we'll burn it by the hillside."

"In aid of what?"

"What sort of question is that? It'll be our final act of defiance and bonding here."

"You seem to have convinced yourself that the soldiers won't burn us instead."

"None of these beer thieves will venture near that hill in the dead of night."

"And what makes you think that anyone else, apart from Shanka and his fellows, will do such a thing?"

"Because there's nothing to lose. In any case, I'll get Shanka to act as a guide. I'll also invite Ignatius, Razaki, Segi, and Haile."

"I'll come along, sure. But, sometimes, I can't help wondering: what is the value of a symbol in these bleak times?"

"Symbols are dreams at work, acquiring roots. You and I, what would be the point of our being without such rooted dreams? For what would we have lived – the bar and its profanities or the struggle and its attitudes?"

"Viva the emergency!"

While Ashikodi and Prinzi drank and their voices soared, a crowd assembled at the Church of Maroko. Pastor David had obtained permission from Captain Doom to hold a Resettlement Communion. Many people came because of the expectation that the pastor's pledges would, on that day, be transformed into cash.

"Children of the living God," the suave pastor saluted his congregation. "This is the day that the Great Lord has Himself specially blessed. I stand before you today with glad tidings. On this eve of the departure from Maroko, the Holy Spirit has asked me to disburse His many gifts to everyone here today."

The church shook with wild jubilation.

"In disbursing these gifts, I will follow a new pattern that the Holy Spirit has set out for me. Blessed is he who walks in the path of the Lord, for the fear of God is the beginning of wisdom."

A great stillness descended on the church.

"Fear you not, children of the living God, and walk you in faith always. All are equal before the Lord, so I have been asked to give to everyone here today the same as their neighbor, no more no less. Each person is to receive one million naira."

The congregation became wildly jubilant again – an occurrence that dangerously put a strain on the wooden stilts of the building.

"Receive now, your blessings. Receive it today and forever."

Already schooled on what to do, Quiet and the other churchwardens began to pass round trays of white envelopes. It was the first and the minor disappointment for those who had expected to receive the money in cash. The second and the major letdown was the fact that each envelope contained a check issued by a "Bank of Heaven" with an extraterrestrial address. The excitement transformed into murmurs and hisses. Pastor David licked his lips.

"Children of the living God! Never you doubt the Lord, lest your fate be like that of the children of Israel wandering in the wilderness out of Egypt. The way of the Lord is the way of the spirit.

Believe in the gift, b-e-l-i-e-v-e, and you shall receive. Claim it with faith! On faith resteth all miracles. May you continue to walk in faith."

"*Arise, be enlightened, O Jerusalem,*" he began to read from the Bible, "*for thy light is come, and the glory of the Lord is risen upon thee. For, behold darkness shall cover the earth and a mist the people but the Lord shall arise upon thee and his glory shall be seen upon thee. And the Gentiles shall walk in thy light, and kings in the brightness of thy rising. Lift up thy eyes round about and see: all these are gathered together, they are come to thee. Thy sons shall come from afar and thy daughters shall rise up at thy side. Thou shalt see and abound, and thy heart shall wonder and be enlarged: when the multitude of the sea shall be converted to thee, the strength of the Gentiles shall come to thee....Thy sun shall go dim no more and thy moon shall not decrease. For the Lord shall be unto thee an everlasting light: and the days of thy mourning shall be ended. And thy people shall be all just; they shall inherit the land forever, the branch of my planting, the work of my hand, to glorify me. The least shall become a thousand, and a little one a most strong nation: I, the Lord, will suddenly do this thing in its time.*"

"Praise the Lord! Jerusalem is the city of God. And we are the children of God. We are the new Jerusalemites. Possess your possessions, O children of God, for the Lord has given these things to you. Walk you in faith from this day forward and your life shall never be the same. This the Lord has asked me to tell you."

Ahead of the choir, the pastor began a song:
> It shall be permanent
> It shall be permanent
> What the Lord has done for me
> It shall be permanent

Gradually, the song reached a crescendo that brought a smile to the face of Pastor David as he motioned for the offertory procession to commence. Nevertheless, there were some people who threw their checks on the floor – as Queen did – or who stormed out of the church. There were also some others who picked up the rejected checks and added them to theirs.

While the offertory procession was going on in the Church of Maroko, the Resettlement Board was establishing its presence in the motor park. A queue quickly formed – with Madam Bonus, accompanied by Segi, at the front. The sole female member of the board, and its chairperson, announced the basic requirement: a lease agreement or proof of house ownership. She then told the assembled residents about the new Maroko.

"It's by the Atlantic Ocean, so you can be sure of a healthy sea breeze, instead of the foul stench here from the over-polluted lagoon. Away from the hustle and bustle that living so close to Greater Lagos must mean, you can also be sure of really peaceful days and nights. Some of us, in case you don't know, envy your luck."

Her audience maintained a judicious silence.

Asked to present her documents, Madam Bonus did so silently. The chairperson, Mrs Odukomaiya, studied the papers, and consulted what seemed to be a register.

"The lease is in order. You may be able to get an apartment in the new Maroko."

"But..." Segi cut in.

"Don't interrupt, young woman! As I was saying, you may be able to get an apartment. Are you married?"

"No."

"Divorced?"

"I'm not married."

"Any children?"

"Segi here is my adopted daughter."

"I see. What do you do for a living?"

"I'm a restaurateur," Madam Bonus said.

"What's your restaurant called?"

"Bonus Restaurant. We have special discounts for the poor."

"How long have you been in the business?"

"Twenty-one years."

"Really? Well, I'm sure restaurants will be needed in the new Maroko. As a spinster, you're supposed to get a single-room apartment, but I'll make an exception and give you a bigger place."

Madam Bonus thanked the woman, collected the necessary relocation papers and hurried away with Segi.

"Next?"

Haile tendered his documents. Mrs Odukomaiya studied the man intensely.

"As far as I can see," she said at last, "your lease is in order. But...you are a Rastafarian, I suppose?"

"Yes, I am."

"What is that really about – apart from carrying unkempt hair?"

"Rastafarianism is a way of life, madam. It means all people is brothers."

Prinzi, who had left Ashikodi at his bar to queue behind Haile, nudged the Rastafarian.

"I see. 'All people is brothers,' eh? What is your occupation?"

"I sell records."

"What sort of records?"

"I only play and sell records by Fela Anikulapo-Kuti."

"Really? Why?"

"Because the music is popular with expatriates, who are his main clients," Prinzi chipped in.

"Don't interrupt, please. Are you married?"

"No."

"Any children?"

"No."

"And parents?"

"Of course."

"Still alive?"

"Both."

"Where?"

"In the village."

"Well, we can't assign you a place in the new Maroko. You do not meet the character requirement. You are free, of course, to appeal the decision of this board."

"To whom?" wondered Prinzi.

"The Governor of Lagos, His Excellency Colonel Raji Omo-ale."

"I protest!" Haile objected loudly. "This is a gross violation..."

Seeing Mrs Odukomaiya bring out a whistle from her pocket, Prinzi nudged Haile out of the queue. "Remember the emergency," he whispered.

"Next?" Mrs Odukomaiya called out, putting away the whistle.

Prinzi placed his papers in front of her.

"All in order," she said after inspection. "And what are you, Mr Prinzi? I have this feeling that I've come across your name before. Have you been in the news?"

Prinzi laughed carefully. "Certainly not. A case of mistaken identity, I'm sure. To answer your first question, I run a snack shop."

"You do? And what do you sell in your snack shop?

"Confectioneries, baked..."

"And alcoholic beverages?"

"Well..."

"Ah, I've got it. Yes, I've seen your name before. You wrote a short story called 'Fingerprints' or something like that – published in *The Times*."

What an irony, Prinzi thought, for Mrs Odukomaiya, of all people, to remember his only published literary work – and on such a day!

"I found the story intriguing. You are a writer then?"

Prinzi would not deny the title under any circumstance. "Yes, I am. However, I've only written that one story."

"A writer who runs a 'snack bar' in Maroko? That's

suspicious. Are you a spy?"

"Madam, that's not possible," Prinzi said solemnly.

With Prinzi's heart racing, Mrs Odukomaiya held whispered consultations with her colleagues.

"Mr Prinzi, we're going to assign you a small room, with the caution that the government reserves the right to eject miscreants and propagandists without notice. With only one short story to your credit, you may reasonably be regarded as a failed writer. I advise that you maintain that status quo."

Prinzi collected his relocation documents with a murderous look in his eyes.

"Next?"

Mama Badejo stepped forward, hands clasped together.

"Your papers, madam."

She tendered a rent receipt from her squatter-landlord. Mrs Odukomaiya adjusted her glasses, looked at the receipt, and consulted her register.

"Case dismissed. Not eligible. Next?"

"Madam, abeg. Wetin I wan' do now, me and my children? My first husband die for civil war wey e dey fight for Nigeria. The second one die like mystery. Na *akara* I dey fry since. How you go look old woman like me come throway me for roadside? How I wan' do?" the woman pleaded tearfully.

"My hands are tied, madam. You may appeal to the Governor of Lagos, His Excellency Colonel Raji Omo-ale."

"How I wan 'ppeal to governor, eh, poor woman like me? Abeg..."

The whistle appeared once more. Mama Badejo was gently led away by Quiet, Centigrade, and Idi. While they led the wailing woman away, World Bank, just arriving at the scene, walked to the head of the queue and stood before Mrs Odukomaiya. A stocky man, his face bore the signs of several knife fights and one finger was missing from his left hand – shot off, some claimed, in a gunfight that no one in Maroko had actually witnessed. Although he was known to possess neither a lease agreement nor any proof of house ownership but was perennially engaged in intemperate disagreements with Centigrade, his squatter-landlord, no one in the queue nudged him or protested his audacity.

"Go and join the queue," Mrs Odukomaiya told him icily.

"Wetin be my own with queue? Wey my own paper? Na me be the World Bank wey you dey hear about all over the world."

The four members of the board blew their whistles almost simultaneously. A volley of gunshots from the direction of the main barricade was the immediate response. The stocky man realized his reputation was at stake. As he stretched his hairy hand toward Mrs Odukomaiya, four armed soldiers appeared.

"Hold it! If you move, you're dead."

World Bank hesitated for only a moment, then he bolted away. The soldiers, who had strict instructions not to fire at anyone except if so commanded by their superior, let him go.

"Now, identify yourselves," one of the soldiers ordered those in the queue. "And if you have no correct business here, better vanish quick quick."

Three quarters of the people in the queue melted away.

Later in the day, the evening edition of *The Echo* carried a front-page story headlined "Mayhem in Maroko." Written by Maina, whose appointment as the editor of the paper had been announced earlier in the day, the report upset many people in Maroko. "In that festering slum called Maroko, an attempt, led by a local fat cat, to disrupt the laudable work of the Resettlement Board was this afternoon skillfully stopped by security operatives enforcing an inevitable state of emergency..."

Ashikodi brought a copy of the paper to Prinzi's Café.

"Maina!" exclaimed Prinzi after reading the story.

"World people!" said Ashikodi.

"He has even arrogated to himself the status of a Maroko expert, perhaps because he comes this way once in a while with a stiff nose. Look at this! Maina hasn't been seen in Maroko since the governor's visit, so he must have written this based on hearsay."

"And the pathetic omniscience of a newly promoted editor

in a government echo of a newspaper. He even referred to World Bank as a local fat cat."

"Maina and his faulty metaphors! The so-called World Bank is a hyena."

"But...the man has grown roots here, which is certainly not a plus for Maroko."

"In the whole of this 'festering slum,' to quote that blasted Maina, there's not a single police station. People like World Bank are monsters waiting for this sort of climate to fully bare their fangs. You know, there's this story the man likes to tell about the time he was a bus driver, which was when he was named World Bank – because of his extravagance. It's a convention to stop halfway through the journey for the passengers to eat in roadside cafeterias in confluence towns. He would grab his microphone and bellow: 'Hallo passengers! Hallo passengers! We go stop, *abi* make we dey go?' Predictably, the passengers would clamor for a stopover. 'So, make we dey go, *abi*?' World Bank would bellow once more and step on the accelerator. The man must have always been a sadist. This is the man Maina writes about as if he were a local celebrity."

"Forget the Mainas of this world meanwhile. It's time to set out."

"You mean you got Shanka to lead us to the hill?"

"That's the handiwork of Ignatius."

"How?"

"Oh, he's friendly with Epi Eye. I whispered to him to whisper to her. She's virtually got Shanka around her fingers."

"Must have been one hell of a whisper."

"What has Shanka got to lose? He will never hunt there again. Come on, man. Is Haile coming? I haven't seen him today."

"He'll meet us at the foot of the hill. Three is now 'congregation,' you know. Haile's been despondent since his Rastafarian tangle with the Resettlement Board. I've invited him to stay with me. Mighty oaks from little acorns sometimes grow, you know."

"A cliché unworthy of Prinzi."

Prinzi winced. "Let's go. I'll tell you the story of that little Odukomaiya Resettlement Board on the way."

When they got to the foot of the hill, both Shanka and Ignatius were already there. While Shanka had a locally made gun, a bag slung over his shoulder, and a torch strapped to his forehead, Ignatius had a large sack that contained masks, an effigy, and a lantern.

Segi and Haile joined the four just as the beginning of the curfew was announced over a microphone and Maroko lay in state.

"Segi the Lola!" Ashikodi lit up.

"It's a pity Razaki is not here with us," noted Prinzi.

"Razaki is going to be unhappy that he missed this adventure," Haile said.

"It's not an adventure," Ashikodi told the group. "This is what I had planned for the whole Maroko, but who could have foreseen this accursed state of emergency? Shanka, we're waiting."

The hunter led the way through a narrow track. With each step, the darkness deepened and the sounds of the forest diversified. The journey continued – with Segi gripping Ashikodi's hand and Haile at the rear casting suspicious glances behind and all about him – until it finally terminated at a pond.

"Na here we dey call Mermaid Pond," said Shanka. He explained that it was the best spot for shooting at the luminous eyes of animals at night. "Na here mamiwota dey appear sometimes, but you no go fit take ordinary eye see am."

"Jah lives!" Haile exhaled.

"Perfect," Ashikodi said. "Here, the water meets the land and the air is all about us. Now, we light a fire and we have the four elements with us."

"Perfect for the 'Roko," sneered Prinzi, who was ill at ease.

"And for Segi. Who can deny her?"

"I suspect blackmail here."

"Please, Prinzi, we'll argue another time. Now, Ignatius, we're waiting."

Ignatius emptied the contents of the sack on the floor of the forest. Ashikodi provided a crayon and boldly named the effigy, then smeared it with a substance he said would ensure it burned without ceasing. He struck a match and lit the effigy. Each person then chose a mask. "This is Razaki," Ashikodi said as he stuck a mask, upright, into the ground. "And now we form a circle around the burning Omo-ale, because circles are magical. And now we sit on the grass, barefoot, holding hands, because this is a ritual of truth and oneness."

"Is this a voodoo party?" Haile asked.

"My friends," began Ashikodi, "this is our last night in Maroko forever. I know enough about the system to know they'll never let us return, so I thought we should hold this ceremony of reaffirmation. The law is not on our side, but the law is not always just. There is a Maroko of flesh and blood, which we all know, but there is also a larger Maroko of the spirit, of which we're all residents. And the fate of Maroko – the two Marokos – will haunt us all. We are the Seven Fingers of our imagination, because to imagine is to be. And tonight is a ritual of strength through which we strengthen one another for the trials ahead. I am not afraid to dream. Tonight is a Great Dream, and better it is to be defeated than never to dream and dare.

"Because there is an ancient kinship between the dream and the mask, we have carved our own masks. It's also a world of masks. All power derives and sustains itself by masking its weaknesses. But the mask was also the facility with which our ancestors expanded reality and invented their pantheon. So, tonight let us pledge to expand our individual selves by committing ourselves once more to our collective cause.

"Maroko has happened to us. We have to make that count – tomorrow, the day after, and ever after. In this environment of forms and presences, and at this point in our lives, we can see anew that which our reality prompts us toward – and beyond. Now, we put on our masks..."

Like him, each person put on a mask.

"I dream a world. I dream a world of unlimited goodwill."

Segi: "I dream a world of love and peace, without a poverty of opportunity."

Prinzi: "I dream a world of freedom – the freedom to be."

Haile: "Soon come for I and I."

Shanka: "Better dey come."

Ignatius the Hunchback: "We will walk on the waves and we will not sink."

"To dream is to see, to be. Maroko is where the sun sets. Maroko will also, in due time, be where the sun rises. I see the Maraki on the rooftop. Facing the north, she salutes: 'To the people of Maroko, greetings.' Facing the east: 'To the people of Maroko, greetings.' Facing the south, she salutes: 'To the people of Maroko, greetings.' And facing the west: 'To the people of Maroko, greetings.' Now, we put away our masks and plant them in a circle around the burning effigy. This is the end and the beginning."

For a long time, they sat still around the burning effigy, holding hands, each person deep in meditation.

"You know, you're really something, the 'Roko," Prinzi said eventually. "After tonight, nothing can save you from starring in the great Maroko novel."

"Me, I've rediscovered him," said Segi.

"I've always regarded him as a priest without an altar," Haile said. "And he has made me remember Bob Marley's 'Redemption Song': *Emancipate yourselves from mental slavery; none but ourselves can free our minds.*"

"Maroko no go complete without its Ashikodi," Shanka added.

"Ashikodi's Seven Fingers must be the seven innermost names of the river known only to the most devout fishermen."

"Where the river meets the shore, the waves are in ascent," said Ashikodi. "So, too, where the Maroko of flesh and blood meets the Maroko of the spirit. Ignatius, a picture of the masks around the effigy will be a good parting shot. Good for the front page too, I believe."

Eight

The bulldozers came at dawn, just as the curfew ended. Their arrival punctuated Captain Doom's final announcement: "Good morning, Maroko. You are to note that the deadline in the eviction notice by His Excellency, the Governor of Lagos, Colonel Raji Omo-ale, expired one second ago. Officially, therefore, Maroko no longer exists. This is a final warning."

More than the announcement, the tremor caused by the bulldozers alerted many of the residents to the imminent demolitions.

In Prinzi's Café, the proprietor had just seen off the other members of the previous night's communion.

"You're very composed this morning," Haile said as he came back into the bar, looking harassed.

"One must learn to smile, regardless."

"You haven't begun to pack yet?"

"Not yet. I'm still steeling myself to begin. You know, it's difficult to believe that this is, indeed, happening."

"You better hurry up before the bulldozers get here. I understand they're wrecking the marketplace right now."

"You mean they're really pulling down houses with bulldozers? On Christmas Eve, of all days!"

"I understand they're also horsewhipping people and casually breaking a few heads. It appears they want to bury Maroko with as many human heads as possible. Today is Christmas Eve. For Maroko, however, it is the Day of Death, and death comes with pain."

"You know, Haile," Prinzi said as he regarded the Rastafarian, "you've got poetry in your soul. Sometimes."

"Here you are crashing into yourselves in search of enlightenment, Ashikodi said weakly from the doorway. "Outside, the world has ended. I am the first ghost of this apocalypse."

Both were surprised by his return – and bloody face.

"Ashikodi!" Haile and Prinzi cried in unison. "What happened to you?"

Ashikodi came into the room, steadying himself. Prinzi hurried behind his bar and came back with a bottle of beer and a napkin.

"What are you up to?" Haile asked. "What's he supposed to do with a beer and a napkin?"

"The napkin – to wipe the face with. The beer – to wet the napkin and then the throat. I'm sure the 'Roko, flesh or spirit, still knows his beer."

"The things you think of, Prinzi!"

"Oh, the combination is inspired," said Ashikodi as he wiped his face with the napkin, wet with alcohol, and then took a large gulp from the bottle.

"What happened to you?"

"I was on my way home, having taken leave of Segi at the door of the Bonus Club. Oh, Segi the Lola! In the marketplace, bulldozers were at work pulling down buildings. Out of nowhere darts out Mar, acting as if destined to be crushed by one of those predetermined bulldozers. I darted after it and managed to pull it away in time, just in time. That was my crime. One of these ubiquitous soldiers set upon me with a horsewhip, no question asked. Unbelievably, salvation came in the form of Captain Doom. He cautioned the soldier against assaulting civilians and ordered me away from the scene, by which time Mar had long since vanished."

"You mean Captain Doom does have a heart at all?"

"I've always suspected that, despite his bluster. The soldier was trying to say something about my attempting to commit suicide, but he gave him a hard look. Even for Captain Doom, today isn't a day for tribunals of words."

"This is terrible. You mean you let a little soldier get away with tearing some flesh off your face?" Prinzi said with a mischievous glint in his eyes.

"As if you would have torn the soldier's head off his

shoulder if you were the victim," Haile said to Prinzi.

"Which he may still be. In any case, we're all victims already – the soldiers, the bulldozer drivers, the masses. The rich and powerful are readying their goats and turkeys for their Christmas meals while Maroko is being ground into the dust. But the foolish soldier that whipped me doesn't know how much trouble he's created for himself until I get to my island and curse him with a coconut in my left hand."

Both Prinzi and Haile burst into laughter.

"And what difference would that make?"

"You just wait, or would you rather change places with the soldier? Prinzi, another beer wouldn't be a bad idea on a day like this. What do you think, Haile?"

"I'm off, to throw my things together before the bulldozers move the earth under my feet." And he took his leave, with Ashikodi muttering about Rastafarians who did not understand that "I and I" meant "I, my brother's keeper."

One, who had gone to see what was happening, entered then. Her headgear was tied around her waist in the manner of one coming from a battlefront, an impression heightened by her dust-coated feet.

"Good morning, Mr Ashikodi," she greeted.

The salutation brought a smile to Prinzi's face. "Mr Ashikodi, hmm? An interesting title."

"Well met in daylight," said Ashikodi, ignoring Prinzi.

"I knew you wouldn't resist the temptation, Mr Ashikodi," Prinzi chided him.

"You keep bantering as if the earth isn't quaking," retorted Ashikodi. "It won't be long before the bulldozers get here, Mr Prinzi."

"That's true," said One. "We have to finish packing, Prinzi. These devils mean business. One of their bulldozers has just crushed Mar to death."

"What?" exclaimed the two men.

"Out there, they're saying that the whole commotion must

have unhinged its mind."

"One would have thought a monkey could withstand this noisy and destructive monkey business," Prinzi said. "What a day!"

Prinzi had already made arrangements the previous day to evacuate his property. He now began to fervently hope that the truck driver with whom he had an understanding would arrive at his bar before the bulldozers.

In the marketplace, the pace of destruction had begun to slow down when Centigrade was carried away. He had attempted to dislodge one of the bulldozer drivers, and the soldiers had given him a punishing beating. For the quack doctor, the day had begun very badly. He had been rudely awakened from an erotic dream – in which he had managed to get Segi into his bed – by a disturbance next door. World Bank was the only tenant in the three-bedroom hovel where Centigrade also had his consulting room and bedroom. The relationship between the landlord and his tenant was one of the well-known stories in the settlement – the disagreements over rent payments and the ejection notices that World Bank threateningly threw back at Centigrade.

As soon as he awoke, unhappily, Centigrade knew that something unusual was going on in the next room. He was already used to World Bank's sinister goings and comings. This morning was different in that World Bank was yelping as if he was being beaten to death. Just as Centigrade was about to hallelujah his tenant's pains, he heard the sound of heavy boots coming toward his door. He bolted out of bed as the door caved in under the impact of a savage kick. Two soldiers carrying guns and horsewhips filled the room.

"Wetin you still dey do here?" one snapped at Centigrade. "You wan' make we waste you?"

As the addressee's jaw dropped open in alarm, his pet monkey bolted from the room.

Not deigning to speak to him again, one of the soldiers pushed the window open and began to fling his property out while the other seized him and dragged him outside where a bulldozer was already waiting to ground the hovel into the dust. The disturbance in the other room had ceased by now, but World Bank was nowhere to be seen. His property had also been dumped outside the house. Comprehension dawned on Centigrade as the bulldozer began to advance on his house the moment the soldiers vacated it. The squatter-landlord could not help it. His knee gave way and he sat on the ground and began to wail while the house shattered with a rattle at the first impact, thrashing like a decapitated fowl.

For a long time, Centigrade did not stir. The house had meant more to him than just a rudimentary shelter constructed with mud, rotting timber, and used zinc. He had grown up not knowing his father. When his mother remarried in his tenth year, his stepfather had made it clear by his actions that he was not welcome. So, he ran away. In his wanderings, he had learned how to dance for a living. When he eventually became a quack doctor as a means of survival, he had acquired a monkey as a dancing companion.

Dancing in diverse markets and always on the move, sometimes only one step ahead of the police or enraged clients, he had dreamed of one day building a house, any sort, a place where he would find the peace and welcome that had long eluded him. As his concoctions got better, he began to make a little more money and was able to stop for longer periods in the same town. In Maroko, where he had finally decided to settle, he had danced about in improvised consulting rooms for years before he was able to realize his dream. For a long time, he would not accept a tenant. When he eventually did, he realized only too late that he had been deceived into admitting *wahala* into his home.

The trouble was in the form of a man, World Bank, who in the early days spoke of his "business connections" with reckless charm. But the house meant so much to its owner that even though he severally threatened to "abandon" it because of his "evil tenant," he could never bring himself to do so.

When the talk about erasing Maroko off the map began, Centigrade prayed that the tale would be disproved like others before it. Instead, his house, which was behind the market, ended up as one of the first casualties of the tale being made flesh. As he sat pondering his fate and began to take some interest in what was going on around him, he understood why the demolition of his home had not drawn the whole of Maroko. Similar demolitions were the norm in the settlement that morning. Wondering what had become of Mar, he got up and began to wander around the rubble of the demolished building. "And You, God, why are You so quiet?" he asked again and again. He was about to start looking for his pipe when one of the bulldozers – having completed its mission on that row – rumbled past him on its way to the next street. Reflexively, he hurled himself at the driver. The last thing he saw, as a blow sent him sprawling to the ground, was the butt of an army rifle.

As soldiers carried Centigrade away, his story crossed the street and became the conversation in front of the nearby Bonus Club where Madam Bonus, Segi, and Ray were on the verge of departure. Not one to be caught unawares if she could help it, Madam Bonus had already sent off her girls and property in hired trucks. Outside the Bonus Club, another truck waited.

"I think we should get going, madam, while we still can," Segi said once more. "These soldiers and bulldozer drivers may get tired of knocking down houses and set on people."

"They're here already and we've waited this long. I'll wait...until I see the end."

"Look, madam!" cried Ray. "They're taking away Dr. Swallow. Looks as if he's dead."

"I don't think so. That's not the way they carry corpses, when they bother to do so, and today doesn't seem like such a day."

"First, they carried away that scum, World Bank, in almost the same manner. Now, Dr. Swallow. Let's go, madam."

"Be patient, Segi. Two of the bulldozers are coming this way now. This house you're looking at was a dream come true. I saw its beginning. I will see its end."

"You want to be haunted by it?"

"It will haunt me anyway."

"Perhaps we could come back later," suggested Ray.

"That's not the same thing."

"Let's make way for the bulldozers then. It'll soon be over."

It was. With the three looking on and Madam Bonus averting her head with each impact of metal on cement, the Bonus Club came tumbling down.

"Sometimes, you know something will happen but you don't believe it until it has actually happened," Madam Bonus muttered weakly, clasping Segi.

"Please, let's go now, madam. I'll lose my mind if I stay here much longer."

"This world! I'll just pick some rubble, then we'll leave. You never know, someday we may be able to throw them at that bastard monkey, Omo-ale. That will be some kind of justice."

"In this world, madam, there's no justice," said Ray, fingering the knife scar on his face. "Even an eye for an eye isn't justice. It only expands the damage."

"This world!" said Madam Bonus in a drained voice. And she broke into tears.

"Farewell, Maroko," Segi muttered as she led the woman away. "Farewell, broken lives; your hearts will beat again."

A silent Ray nodded an "Amen" and the three departed.

Not so Mama Badejo. She had managed to drag herself and her children away from the ruins of the one room they had lived in, in a house near Centigrade's. Now, they squatted in front of the demolished stall where she used to fry beancakes as if contemplating the end of the world and invoking a dead god from tablets of ash.

"Na which kin' *yeye* country be this?" she wailed, with her children as silent witnesses, their attention often distracted by the mayhem around them. "Everyday na so so *wahala*. How ordinary woman like me wan' survive for this country now with all these children to look after? When my husband wan' go fight *yeye* civil war for Nigeria, I dey hold am like masquerade e be like say I no know wetin I dey do. They kill am for war front, still Nigeria no bellyful. This country wan' kill us all finish. The second one, e die just like that. How we wan' do this life now, eh? Where I wan' start from? Look all my children. This one na only head e be, this one na only belly, this one na only neck, this one only leg. How they wan' do for this world? God in heaven above, which day You wan' fulfil Your promise to end this world? All these *orishirishi* wickedness, all these surplus suffering, they never do for You to judge? *Haba*! God, na only You remain for me. You must answer me today."

She began a song:
Let him be my God
God that answereth by fire...

Gradually, more people joined them – Idi with his wife and four children, each buckling under a load; Ignatius pushing his truck almost overflowing with all sorts of things and muttering fiercely under his breath; Goomsi with his expensive-looking bags. Each was a portrait of misery. None of them had been given a place in the new Maroko "wonderland." None had secured any alternative accommodation.

"Goomsi, where you get all these fine bags from?" Idi asked.

"Na my madam cast offs. If person serve king finish, if e no get im own crown, e go at least get feather."

"But how she go cast off these fine bags when man never fit afford ordinary sack?"

"Na so world be. Some people tall, some short."

"Some dey give order, some dey suff-e-r. Why God create this world like this sef?"

"Abeg, leave God first. Where E dey too far. You think say this Maroko wey no dey for Omo-ale map go dey for God own?"

"I know that my redeemer liveth," Mama Badejo cut in with a sentence often used by Pastor David.

"Amen," chimed Idi's wife, Iya Idi, a bony woman who had been a laundress in Maroko. She was known to defer to her husband and hardly ever volunteered an opinion in his presence. That morning, however, she appeared to have become a bit liberated by circumstances. Nevertheless, Idi glared at her as if daring her to chime another "Amen."

Goomsi, who was not in the mood for conversation, moved a few steps away and began to chew his fingernails absentmindedly. When Alhaja Osunwunmi had locked up her house the previous day, he had moved in with Queen at the Green Parrot Hotel. That morning, Queen, who had secured a room in another brothel in another part of Lagos, had moved out, and he had begun to wander around Maroko. He did not know what to do with himself or where to go next. Although he had done several odd jobs, he had not mastered any. As he sat biting his fingernail, he wondered whether returning home was not his best option. He quickly dismissed the thought.

Goomsi's thoughts were interrupted by a dry laugh from Ignatius, who had been sitting morosely by his truck, on which was boldly written: "To be a man is not a day's job."

"The first day Ashikodi sat down with Segi at the Bonus Club, he could not look her in the face," the hunchback said to no one in particular. "He kept filling her ears with sweet nothings, but he would not look her in the face. Could not. She was puzzled. 'Is it that it's your style or is it that you're uncharacteristically shy that you don't look people in the face when you're talking to them?' she asked him. Still with an averted face, he told her: 'The truth is that you're so beautiful that I'm afraid if I looked you in the face I would be blinded by your beauty and I might lose my mind.' When he told me the story, I educated him. You see, it's not the fault of the hunchback that he carries in his hump the secrets of the universe. I told him that if he looked her in the face seven times he would be cleansed enough to be worthy of her. It's in the Bible, too. The leper, Naaman, he washed in the river Jordan seven times and he became clean, *abi*? With each dip, he invoked one of the seven secret names of the river known only to the most devout fishermen. You see, the soul of a fisherman – a true initiate, that is – is as deep as the rivers. The same thing is happening to us now and to that devil Omo-ale, sort of. He has destroyed Maroko and invoked the first hell on himself. What he needs now is six more destructions and he'll be clean enough to be the chief superintendent in hell, in its seventh and worst firepit where Satan attends to coup plotters. Look you people sef, you don't even know anything. You're just crying for yourselves. Pity Omo-ale! He has some horrendous monkeying to do in hell." He gave another dry laugh, jumped down from where he sat, and departed – pushing his truck and muttering fiercely once more.

"Phew!" Idi whistled. "Today na today. Any craze wey people no craze for Maroko today, they no go ever craze am again. See as Ignatius head don turn finish so-tey e dey do interpreter inside burning bush."

"I know that my redeemer liveth," Mama Badejo said again. Iya Idi's reflexive "Amen" was frozen by a look from her husband.

"Mama Badejo, this your redeemer wey you know, e know you at all?"

"Thou shall not take the name of the Lord in vain."

"I hear that Madam Bonus caught a thief, an old man, stealing something from the Bonus Club. Unlike her, she did not punish him. She actually said a prayer for him instead, asking God to forgive him and please bless him. On a day like this, prayers must have a special appeal. Maybe if I could pray..."

"Make we pray together, Brother Goomsi. And you, God in heaven, you must answer us today." Gathering her children together, Mama Badejo linked her hand with Goomsi's and began to pray with growing frenzy. At some point, Iya Idi overcame her dread, gathered her children together too and joined in. Idi also managed to put his anger against God in abeyance and joined the group – just before Mama Badejo ended the prayer.

"Oh Lord, you are our light and our salvation. If you do not lead us out of this darkness, you will surely lose your purpose. Thank you, Lord, for I know you have answered our prayers.

Thank you, Father."

She was about to start a song when the bulldozers began to converge around them. Their alarm became uneasy comprehension when the bulldozers came to a halt and the drivers – mostly young men incongruously clad in white overalls already browning with dust – climbed down, each carrying a lunch bucket. They sat beside one of the bulldozers and began to eat out of their buckets. The two groups ignored each other. It was not too long, however, before one of the drivers crooked a finger at Idi's youngest daughter and held up a piece of yam. As the girl began to move toward him, another driver flung a piece of meat in her direction. It fell on the grass. The girl scampered after it. An enraged Idi sprang up, reached her with a few bounds, gave her a knock that sent her reeling, picked up the piece of meat and flung it back at the offerer. He then dragged the sobbing girl back to the fold.

"Stupid thing! You never see yam or meat before for your life na im you wan' eat Satan food, *abi*? Which kin' stupid children I get sef?"

"Oga, make you calm down," the man who had crooked a finger appealed across the invisible divide.

"Who be your oga? God forbid! You no see Captain Doom call am oga, you no see Omo-ale who be your master? Young man like you no see better thing take your life do na to destroy other people. Look you, na poor people like me and you na we be our worst enemies. You demolish my house finish, that one no do you. Now you wan' rub pepper inside the wound. No let me swear for you, *oloshi*."

"Joe," the man who had flung the piece of meat called out to his colleague. "Better be careful."

Joe was not to be deterred. "My friend," he said to Idi, "I'm only doing my work. If I don't do it, somebody else will. Nothing personal. I know a couple of people in Maroko myself. All of us, we're in God's hands."

"Wetin I even dey do dey talk to this animal? All of you, make una carry our load make we comot here quick quick before

I craze proper. I pity this God, true. Even animals and devils dey call Im name too. Come on, quick quick!"

"I know that my redeemer liveth," said Mama Badejo as she and her children went off with the Idis.

Lacking both a will and a compass, Goomsi sat staring into space, wondering with one of the many corners of his mind that afternoon if the trains still arrived at Goom Station. Joe crooked a finger at him. He blinked. Walking like a somnambulist, he crossed the invisible divide.

A meal was also what Shanka and Epi Eye shared at about the same time. Shanka had returned to his lodgings that morning with a big appetite. It was as if he had known he would, for he had procured a large grasscutter and some rice the previous day.

"You no go find person wey go buy this grasscutter, Shanka, or we no go cook am eat?" Epi Eye, who had moved in with him, had asked. "This one wey you dey keep am for tomorrow, tomorrow na *wahala* day-o."

"Unless you wan' do the cooking yourself, I no dey in the mood to cook today."

Cooking was one of the things Shanka prided himself on being able to do well. Epi Eye, on the other hand, regarded cooking as a dreadful chore.

"You know say me I no sabi cook, Shanka, *abi* you dey laugh me?" she replied. "Tomorrow, I go help you as I fit – that is, if they never flush us out by that time."

"No worry yourself, Epi Eye," Shanka said smugly. "Me, Shanka, I don dey pass that stage."

"Na wa-o! You don dey talk like big man, ever since that car begin come find you."

"Better dey come, Epi Eye."

As the two feasted on the pepper soup and jollof rice Shanka had prepared that morning, the hunter reiterated the prophecy.

"I don dey talk am since," said Epi Eye. "E go hard you to marry, Shanka, because which woman fit dey cook food wey go impress you when you yourself na five-star chef?"

"That one no be problem. I go employ better cook for that. My wife no need to enter kitchen at all."

"Eh-he! You don dey make me fear as you dey talk, *abi* you don win lottery you no wan' tell me?"

"You know say me I no dey play lottery. Shanka no be Quiet or Centigrade. But my way don dey open, *abi* you wan' talk say I never tell you that?"

"What of your Epi Eye?"

"No worry yourself. I don tell you make you wait for me for New Maroko. I get to travel first, then I go come that side. And when I come, e no go be small arrival-o."

"This your travel, you sure say no be wife you wan' go marry?"

Shanka chuckled. "Maybe, but that one no mean say I no go do you well. No worry yourself."

"Where you wan' travel go, and when you dey return?"

"You never hear say na too much knowledge make tortoise break im shell?"

Epi Eye opened her mouth to say something, thought better of it and concentrated instead on wolfing down the leg of a grasscutter.

"So, na so Maroko end be that?" she said when she finished eating. "I go miss this jungle, true. I wonder how this New Maroko wan' be."

"I go miss the bush myself. Hunting dey my blood. But as life be, when one door close another go open."

"Na the kin' thing wey that Ashikodi dey talk."

"Shanka and Ashikodi na the same thing?"

Epi Eye snuggled close to him and began to caress him. "Of course, Shanka na my big masquerade," she cooed in his ears. "But you think say God go forgive that Governor Omo-ale?"

"Wetin the man do? All these people wey dey cry today say governor don kill them some go turn around later to bless am because their lives go better."

"And plenty go curse am more."

"Maybe. No gain without loss."

"Time..." Epi Eye rolled the word on her tongue, fluttering her eyelashes. "Time for an Epi Eye special forget-me-not."

Her caresses became more arousing. Shanka, who knew full well the sexually satisfying rock and roll that an Epi Eye special meant, responded with passion.

"I came to Maroko with nothing and I dey leave with nothing, except you," he said afterward. "That one go show you how special you dey to me."

"You no go carry your things?"

"Carry wetin? All these na the old Shanka."

Epi Eye had only one rucksack. As she explained, her occupation did not encourage a lot of baggage. Shanka helped her carry the bag as they left.

They arrived at the marketplace as the bulldozers were rumbling out of Maroko. The extent of the demolition on that first day brought them to an abrupt halt. In the entire area before their stunned gaze, only one building, Faith Villa, was still standing – like a solitary resurrection in an infinite city of the dead. It had always been the tallest building in Maroko. Now, it was the tallest building in the world – a universe of rubble.

"Jesus Christ of Nazareth!" exclaimed Epi Eye.

"Na wa-o. See as that Maraki Palace just stand like one mighty erection."

Without any warning, the heavens opened and it rained "Noah's flood," the description later popularized by Ashikodi. As the two scurried toward Faith Villa, Shanka was struck by an old man sitting by a pile that must have been his hovel – like a stone Buddha oblivious of the rain. He was plaintively singing "O come, all ye faithful, joyful and triumphant." The sight was so arresting that Shanka paused before the rain drove him forward. The song followed him. *O come ye, O come ye to Bethlehem.*

Book 3
New Maroko

Nine

That first week, between Christmas Eve and New Year's Day, was the most chaotic. The uprooted men, women, and children that poured into New Maroko realized early that they had to resettle themselves. The Resettlement Board, which had promised to be "available" to welcome "genuine" tenants, was nowhere evident. Although numbers, which sometimes corresponded to the ones on the resettlement certificates issued by the Board, had been marked on the doors of some of the houses, there were no keys and the windows were shuttered. That Christmas Eve, therefore, the evictees gradually resigned themselves to the fact that they would have to sleep in the open.

The place was a coastal sprawl. Its gloomy appearance was reinforced by the only enterprise that had existed in the vicinity until then: the incinerator. It stood like a giant totem and cast a pall over its immediate environs. The defective houses the government had built, obviously in a great hurry, were fanned around the incinerator, making it the heart of town.

As the Christmas Eve evictees vainly conjured the Resettlement Board, the evening grew very cold. It was the harmattan season. In their quest for warmth and fellowship, many of the evictees left their sulking corners and converged around the area where Madam Bonus and her girls had set up a tarpaulin tent and lit a bonfire. Ignatius the Hunchback, who had decided to postpone his journey to Coconut Island, had positioned his truck beside the fire and was about to begin one of his Demolition Day monologues.

"It's a world with two legs up in the air, this," he said. "On the day that God created the birds of the air, He created two puzzling creatures: the vulture and the bat. Neither of these fears that which mankind dreads. The bat is not afraid of darkness. But at least the bat does not scorn death. Not so the vulture. It grows fat on the dead and the decaying.

"Then came the night of blinding darkness and evil omens when the bat and the vulture mated. The bat carried the embryo for a long time, then it gave birth to a curious creature that was neither a bat nor a vulture. It had the wings of a bat and the beak of a vulture. It hung upside down like a bat; it flew like a vulture. But it had come into the world blind. It did not see in the day like the bat; it did not see in the night like the vulture. That is the short and complete biography of His Excellency, Colonel Raji Omo-ale, the Governor of Lagos."

The crowd made him tell the tale again.

Segi finally began a song:

> O Lord, let me be in their number
> When the saints go marching in
> When the saints
> When the saints
> Go marching in
> Go marching in
> O Lord, let me be in their number
> When the saints go marching in

"True," said Idi loudly, "e be like say man don lose out for this world. E be like say that heaven na im remain. True."

Iya Idi was so pleasantly surprised that she recited, aloud, her favorite portion of the Bible.

"*In the beginning, God created heaven, and earth. And the earth was void and empty, and darkness was upon the face of the deep. And the spirit of God moved over the waters. And God said: 'Be light made.' And light was made. And God saw the light that it was good; and he divided the light from the darkness. And he called the light Day and the darkness Night. And there was evening and morning one day.*

"*And God said: Let there be a firmament made amidst the water: and let it divide the waters from the waters. And God made a firmament, and divided the waters that were under the firmament, from those that were above the firmament. And it was so. And God called the firmament Heaven. And the evening and morning the*

second day.
"*In the beginning...*
"*In the beginning...*"
The crowd recited along with her.
"For those it saddens that they shall one day die," Goomsi intoned with priest-like gestures, "let them take consolation in the resurrection of the dead."
And the night wore on.
Christmas the next day dawned "in gloomful gray" – Goomsi's favored description. Still, the Resettlement Board did not arrive. Maroko did, however, feature in the news that morning, after the governor's syrupy Christmas message. The broadcaster informed the evictees, and the world, that "Maroko was yesterday demolished after the expiration of the relocation notice given by His Excellency. While the demolition continues, former Maroko residents have since been resettled."
The evictees were stupefied. Besides their personal anguish, there were many touching stories of fellow evictees robbed or brutalized in other ways. Yet the broadcaster had informed them that they had since been resettled.
The arrival of Centigrade further affected their mood. The "justly famous Dr Swallow," as he sometimes loved to describe himself, looked like a scarecrow that morning. But his walk had an unusual swagger.
"Dr Swallow! Dr Swallow!" The crowd cheered at his approach as if he represented an invincible Maroko.
"I have seen the devil," Centigrade announced, "and he does indeed have seven horns. And having seen the devil, I know for a fact now that there is God and that He is good and mighty. If that were not the case, I wouldn't be here today."
"Dr Swallow! Dr Swallow!"
He confirmed that the attitude in the police clinic where he had been treated and at the Central Police Station where he had been taken to answer "a few questions" that morning was similar to the broadcaster's. A few people asked about World Bank.

"That one? He is still alive. He said he's tired of the small time! Why he had to wait until they destroyed my house before going after 'big game,' I don't know. Good rid...dance all the same. I look forward to reading in the papers: 'Ex-Maroko Gangster Meets His Water...loo.'"

His experience and the mood of the people had given the quack doctor a temerity that he did not usually possess. When he tried the door of one of the houses and found it locked, he simply attacked the door until it fell in. He then declared the main apartment his, even though the Resettlement Board had not certified him a legal resident of Maroko.

One moment, there was a stunned silence; the next, there was a mad scramble for rooms and apartments, during which men and women who had been professing community a while ago sometimes set upon one another with near-homicidal intent. All certificates were voided by the scramble. Not a few fights and accidents resulted, with many windows smashed for quicker access. And in some cases, different families laid claim to different parts of the same apartment.

The Resettlement Board, escorted by anti-riot policemen, arrived after Christmas break. It turned New Maroko upside down, throwing out many illegal residents in the process, before setting it aright again on its own terms.

To those whom the board could not redeem their certificates, Mrs Odukomaiya calmly announced: "You are to note, ladies and gentlemen, that all resettlement certificates not already redeemed – and therefore irredeemable – are hereby canceled. The government is not liable under the circumstances. Happy New Year."

The anti-riot policemen raised their guns; the crowd retreated; the Resettlement Board departed. The unfortunate ones, and those whom the board had classified as illegal residents in Maroko, presently set about erecting their own shanties. The result was that the new settlement began to look more like the shantytown that was Maroko than the government-promised New Town.

Gradually, the people became used to their new environment. The nearby Crocodile Island, a relatively small strip of land that was said to harbor an exclusive crocodile museum, and Coconut Island inspired the renaming of the incinerator as Devil's Island. Both the rail and the ocean finger encouraged new modes of livelihood. His three-year exile over, Ignatius the Hunchback happily became a fisherman. Discouraged by the distance that he now had to travel every day to and from the Shelling Hotel, Idi gave up his job and became a sand contractor. Quiet managed to stay awake when it mattered and became a railwayman. The Bonus Club, still located at an arterial junction, added another floor to the bungalow it had been allocated and remained the social center. The Green Parrot Hotel reemerged as Good Evening Hotel. And, once more, the heart of Maroko began to beat.

From his café, which he had modeled after the one in Maroko, Prinzi noted all these with interest. He found the developments so remarkable that he started keeping a diary again, something that he had turned his back on since he wrote his short story. That evening, on New Year's Day, he was making an entry in his diary when Maina entered.

"Happy New Year, Prinzi," the journalist greeted.

Prinzi put away his diary before he scrutinized the visitor as if he were an Unidentified Flying Object.

"Maina! What are you doing here? Considering your jaundiced reports, it's a wonder no one cracked your little skull before you got here."

"I see that you now keep a diary. You must be training yourself to become a journalist someday."

"With someone like you in that profession? No, thank you."

"What are you grumbling about? Your Maroko was nothing but a den of cheap vices. You all should be thankful that someone moved you out of there and purged some undesirable elements in the process."

"Don't tempt me, man, unless you want the imprint of my fist on your face."

"I've just acquired the black belt in karate, and I didn't buy it in the market."

"You've just acquired a black belt, eh? I've had mine for a long time. Better be warned."

"Sure, you got yours in your mother's belly. If I go and write that, you'll claim I misquoted you. You see what I mean?"

"Very very clearly," Prinzi said slowly. "I see now what a distortion machine you've got for a mind."

Leaving Maina, he walked quickly to the door and called across the street: "Haile! Come in here, man. I and I is brothers."

Haile had reestablished his shop opposite Prinzi's Café. When he walked into Prinzi's bar and saw Maina, he came to a halt.

"I need you as a witness," Prinzi told him.

"Cut it out, Prinzi," Maina, who had now served himself a beer and settled into a chair, said. "I don't understand what you're complaining about. Despite being a government-owned newspaper – not the same as a government paper, I must tell you – we published the picture of the burning effigy of the governor that I'm sure either you or Ashikodi sent to us anonymously."

"Oh, you did?" remarked Haile sarcastically.

"With a malicious headline that you, Maina, must have cast: 'Maroko Lunatics Burn Effigy of Governor,'" added Prinzi.

"Not a bad headline," replied Maina. "It's concise. Besides, it probably saved your skin."

"Speaketh the skin-saver," Haile said drily.

"You're learning to talk like Ashikodi, I see, but it doesn't fit. That's not the way a Rastafarian worth his dreadlocks talks. Anyway, I came to find out how you guys are doing. It does seem that Maroko has settled well."

"Go back and tell them that you didn't see us. We've vanished from the face of the earth. I can think of a more concise headline: 'New Maroko Desolate.'"

"Not a bad attempt, but I don't write fiction."

"Yet you think that we have settled well – around an incinerator. You and your government must really conceive of

Maroko as a defeated class, otherwise why would you people move a settlement beside a shit lagoon and fan it around an incinerator?"

"One must apply perspective in these matters. The incinerator wasn't moved here to spite anyone. It was here according to the urban development plan for Lagos. If Maroko hadn't sprung up, illegally, where it did, there wouldn't have been any need for its relocation in the first place. With millions of opportunity prospectors pouring into Lagos, there aren't too many open spaces left for such resettlements. Besides, the incinerator provides employment for some residents. And I understand that the vapor attracts cool air and rainfall. The incinerator certainly has its merits."

Words failed Prinzi.

"If this is the sort of thinking in government circles," Haile said, "I'll be damned. Look, Maina, the world hasn't ended yet and, until the Lion of Judah returns, redemption time still is. Truth heals."

"Holy Moses!" Prinzi exhaled slowly. "Is this the sort of logic you now parrot, Maina? My bar will soon be filling up. When my clients discover who you are, I can't guarantee your safety. I don't even think you're a proper journalist anymore. People like you don't understand the power machine that drives you, and it's your sort that gets fed to the mob to divert its attention and still its cries."

"Talking about power..."

"Not here, *Mr* Maina. There's a sign at the door, even if you can't read it, and it says clearly: Right of Entry Reserved. You better pay up and leave."

"What is this? You want to throw me out?"

"No, I'll incinerate you out if you don't leave this minute."

Haile began to flex his athletic muscles. Maina looked from one to the other. He paid up and left.

"I think I need a bouncer," Prinzi said agitatedly. "I wish that Shanka would show up. Someone like him with a gun at the entrance will discourage people like Maina from coming here."

"You surprise me, Prinzi. Such a spectacle will put you out of business."

Shanka. He arrived in New Maroko some months later chauffeur-driven in a black Mercedes car, the status symbol of the nouveaux riches, accompanied by a truck carrying a prefabricated cabin. The cabin was set up in a corner of the settlement and became his temporary home. It was obvious that the former leader of the hunter's guild in Maroko had become affluent. Not only did he look more robust, he now dressed in rich costumes and owned a cellular phone, another status symbol. His carriage had become rather regal, encouraging the tale that he had been to a School for Princes.

On the evening of his arrival, imported musicians blocked the major street in New Maroko and the residents were treated to a lavish "thanksgiving party," preceded and punctuated by gun salutes.

"I have to thank God, my people, for He has smiled on me at last" was Shanka's only explanation of his sudden wealth.

The next day, work started on his new home. With a large number of workers bustling about, the building was soon completed.

One of the first people to call on Shanka the day after his arrival was Epi Eye, who had been living in Good Evening Hotel. On arrival at the cabin that morning, she was informed that she had to be screened before she could see Shanka. When she was at last admitted into the living room where Shanka sat, she received a cool welcome.

"Ah, Epi Eye, how life now?" Shanka asked.

She went and sat beside him. "Why you dey do me like this, Shanka, *abi* I no reach for you again?"

"What are you talking about?"

"Na so me and you dey do before? You don change toward me."

Shanka made no response.

"Anyway, remember your promise say when you return

everything go dey all right for me, for us. I don tire for this kin' life wey I dey live. I just dey manage myself dey wait for you since."

"No problem. Just give me some time. Better dey come."

"*Abi* better don come your side already? The money wey you spend yesterday alone..."

"Never mind that. I'll settle you soon, but on one condition: you have to leave New Maroko and go far far away. And you must forget everything about me. Your life depends on that."

"Something bad happen, Shanka?"

"In this world, everything is wrong, but we have to make those things that are wrong right. And they are right if they work for us."

"Na where you learn all this merry-go-round grammar? And...wetin sef you think say I wan' talk?"

"Perhaps nothing, but there are things you know that you may not even know that you do. If you start blabbing, nothing or nobody can save you."

"You don dey make me fear. Something bad happen?"

By the oceanfront, where Idi and his fellows had now taken to hanging out at night, Shanka and Epi Eye became the focus of conversation.

"Wetin dey happen sef between that Epi Eye and this new Shanka?" Idi asked no one in particular.

"Wetin you mean?" Orita inquired.

"I hear say sometimes Epi Eye dey go sleep with Shanka for im new house, but e be like say nobody don actually see am dey enter the house. But the wonderful thing be say when people ask this girl about Shanka these days, she go swear – yes, swear – say she no know any Shanka either now or before. You don see that kin' thing before?"

"She has become small meat for the new Shanka," pronounced Ignatius.

"Ah, that Epi Eye no be like small meat-o," Quiet ventured.

"Quiet! Quiet!" hailed the others.

"You think say this new Shanka want the kin' woman the

whole of New Maroko don sleep with?" said Ignatius.

"Except me," declared Goomsi.

"When Queen had you on a leash, maybe. I can't vouch for you now. You see, when Shanka was just a common hunter, maybe he didn't mind too much. Now, he's a big shot, or so he thinks."

"But why the girl dey talk say she no know Shanka when she suppose dey vex for am?"

"I suspect a deal."

"Hmm, but the girl still dey Good Evening Hotel dey struggle."

"Maybe there's been a deal but she hasn't collected or maybe the deal is for her to carry on as before for a certain period."

"But wetin Shanka wan' make deal with Epi Eye for when im no be World Bank type of person?"

"I hear say Epi Eye nearly blind Centigrade when e ask am that kin' question."

"Well, one day we go know. This na New Maroko."

"This na Incinerator Town," said Orita. "And e be like say trouble go soon burst out for that place. The small money wey them dey pay, person no dey see am regularly. I no know the kin' devil wey put man for this *yeye* route so-tey I come dey work for incinerator."

"This incinerator sef, I sure say all the assorted illnesses wey don plenty for New Maroko na im be the cause."

"The thing go don comot some years from our lives already, yet the world just dey look like say this na experiment and we na guinea pigs."

"The world is like an echo. If you howl, then maybe it howls with you. If you fold your hands, then it goes to sleep."

"Na strike na im go solve this matter," Orita said.

"Strike? When people full everywhere wey dey look for work?"

"You never hear the kin' strike wey e be say we no go work and we no go comot?"

"You want to be used for target practice by these 'kill and go' policemen?"

Both Epi Eye and the incinerator also featured in the conversation at Prinzi's Café.

"Isn't it time we solved this incinerator menace once for all?" Razaki posed the question. He now had to travel a shorter distance to Prinzi's Café. "You should do a short story on the problem, Prinzi."

"A short story on the incinerator, why not? But do you sincerely believe that the Governor Omo-ales of this country, with the power to plant and remove incinerators, read short stories? If they did, they probably wouldn't be such carnivores in power. If you go out there right now and move the people to march on the incinerator that will provoke some action immediately."

"All you do is talk, talk, talk."

"And what does your theater do?"

"Hey!" Haile cut in, "I think you fellows are trying to turn a serious matter into another mental exercise. The question still is: how do we tackle this incinerator menace once for all?"

"Well, if we must – it's not an idea I find appealing – we could use Shanka..." Prinzi began.

"Shanka?"

"I understand he's been seen going to and coming from that mysterious Crocodile Island. Some people claim he's helping out with a crocodile museum or something like that. And it's mostly the government that manages museums in this country. Crocodile Island is such an exclusive place that Shanka's access to it suggests that he now has important connections."

"Maybe it's not a bad idea after all," said Razaki.

"Wake up, man," Haile chided. "If Shanka is at all concerned about this problem, why hasn't he done something about it? Have you not noted the location of his house? The fumes can't really trouble him. Besides, why hasn't he helped his former girlfriend?"

"Now, that's curious – not that he hasn't helped her but that she denies any knowledge of him."

"When people start denying relationships that in fact exist, then perhaps they're connected in more ways than other people imagine."

"Let's forget I ever mentioned Shanka's name in the first place. I wouldn't even want to boost his ego by being part of any delegation to him. Man, can you imagine that?"

"May I now inform you gentlemen," Razaki told them, "that I have completed a script called 'Little Christmas,' for New Maroko."

"Little what?"

"What are you up to this time?"

"I don't think that a people resettled around an incinerator have any business celebrating the same festivals as their rulers. So, we should stage a Christmas celebration ahead of the time and we should do so right in front of the incinerator."

"Why?"

"You realize that everyone outside is carrying on as if New Maroko was not resettled around an incinerator? By linking the celebration to the incinerator, we link the incinerator to New Maroko in the consequent press reports, some of which we should influence. Do you realize the effect a picture of people dancing around a belching incinerator situated in a residential district, as if placating an angry god, could have on the world outside? I will not carry this burden of feeling that I belong to a generation that has nothing to say, a generation living in a time of epochal evil but incapable of any large statements."

And so New Maroko came to celebrate Little Christmas, or "Razakimas" as it became known. Ashikodi talked up the festival the most. And he woke New Maroko up that morning with the spectacle of him dancing in the canoe carrying him and some drummers from Coconut Island to New Maroko. The song was an invocation of lightning:

> *Raji 'ale elisia ego-o*
> *Do-o amuma, amuma do-o*

That dawn, by the oceanfront, he put up an impressive "wind dance."

"This Ashikodi don craze finally. They say them dey do Little Christmas, im dey invoke lightning."

"You no know say after God create heaven and earth, the next thing wey Im create na light, *abi* lightning no be light?"

Thereafter, Ashikodi led his drummers to the Bonus Club, this time singing "Segi the Lola." Segi was so moved that she came out and joined in the dance. And the celebration began, boosted by Razaki's arrival dressed as Santa Claus and bearing pebbles – "to stone the incinerator with" – as Christmas presents.

The event turned out well, according to Razaki's script. Shanka was conspicuously absent. According to those who claimed to know, he had traveled out of the settlement that morning on urgent business.

The consequent press reports were mostly favorable, with some newspapers publishing pictures of the celebration in front of the belching incinerator. The tale soon spread that Razakimas had been shown on international television stations. But Maina's report, "Playwright Provokes New Maroko," was so dreadful that it almost blotted out all the others. "Yesterday, two months before the global celebration of Christmas, a self-styled playwright, who is however yet to write any play, attempted to compel the residents of New Maroko to celebrate Christmas prematurely. His attempt provoked a demonstration of outrage marked by mocking songs and dances."

When Ashikodi read the report, he incorporated Maina's name into his song:

Maina efuru uzo-o
Do-o amuma, amuma do-o

What many people considered the reaction of the government came in the form of an announcement by the Resettlement Board, which had transformed into the New Maroko Development Board and set up an office in the area: "All New Maroko residents are to note that, henceforth, all public ceremonies are to be approved by this board. A gate, which will be locked between midnight and six a.m., will be erected at the entrance to New Maroko to facilitate the screening of visitors. All residents will be levied accordingly."

Shortly afterward, Shanka announced the New Maroko Fishing Festival. Two months later, he announced the existence of Kaabiyesi.

Ten

Kaabiyesi!? Both an exclamation and a question.

"That Kaabiyesi, how only am go dey live, with crocodiles, like say na outcast im be? Na so e hate people reach so-tey im get signposts: 'Crocodiles on Guard. No Visitors Allowed'? And that house for im island, the thing just long like say na factory."

"Ashikodi say e no long before they drive us come here na im the house just appear like say na by magic."

"How one person go get that island, wey they even damage the ocean to build, yet the government no dey worry am?"

"Government no be people? They know themselves."

"Wetin be Shanka own for the matter wey e dey do like say the Kaabiyesi na im papa? Since we come here, nothing don appear from that island, suddenly na im cows and horse dey appear like say na from the Kaabiyesi Island. If na only im crocodiles na them full there, where the Kaabiyesi get the cows and the horse from?"

"You no hear Shanka say im and Alhaji Kaita na Kaabiyesi agents? E be like say the story just dey start."

It was not long before Quiet claimed to have seen Kaabiyesi in his sleep. According to his account, he saw a tall man with a halo around his head who beckoned to him with a dazzling smile and said: "I am that I am, the one and only Kaabiyesi. Come to me all ye that labor but are dispossessed."

While some people nodded as if in assent, others derided the tale.

"E be like say all the marijuana wey the poor man dey smoke with Orita dem don dey affect im brain," sneered Centigrade. "He had better come for consultation in my clinic before the matter gets out of hand."

"Eureka!" exclaimed Ashikodi when he heard the story and quickly made for Prinzi's Café, where he met Prinzi and Razaki bantering.

"Eureka!" he exclaimed again.

"What have you discovered this time – more dream visions?"

"I'm sure you must have heard of Quiet's vision of Kaabiyesi. If he can see him, so can I and so can you. We can see him with the eyes of the mind, and we can see him whichever way we choose. And that will probably rile Shanka into an offensive that might give his game away, especially if we see his Kaabiyesi as he would not want him to be seen."

"I hear that Epi Eye has come into sudden wealth and has decided to go home. Maybe she knows something that links Shanka with Kaabiyesi or Alhaji Kaita in such a manner or at such a time that he'd prefer no linkage to be known to have existed. Shanka himself appears to have come into a fabulous personal fortune, as if he's just been paid a huge fee. He has acquired new luxury cars, is said to be building houses in choice areas of Lagos, and he has even taken to smoking cigars. Haile too is on the roll, what with the conversion of his shop to Radio Kaabiyesi. He hardly comes in here these days and is not known to still visit the Shrine."

Haile's Record Shop had indeed become a virtual radio station beginning and concluding each day and sometimes marking every other hour with "special goodwill broadcasts from Kaabiyesi the Benevolent." Haile had expanded the shop and acquired a motorcycle with "Selassie 1" as the only inscription on the license plate.

"Go on, the 'Roko," prompted Razaki. "What is your vision of Kaabiyesi?"

"You can be sure that I'll come up with something so demeaning that Kaabiyesi and his agents will be compelled to react. But that may not happen if the vision is seen as just another New Maroko tale. We should get it into print."

"A book proposal?" asked Prinzi.

"A community newspaper will be more like it, even if all we do is bring out one issue on Kaabiyesi."

"What about funding?"

"I'm sure Razaki here can handle that. He's in the good

books of all sorts of agencies that sponsor his social action theater. Prinzi, you'll be the editor."

"In all, not a bad idea," said Razaki. "We need a group name."

"Something like Project Maroko should suffice."

"I was going to suggest the Seven Fingers," said Ashikodi, "but I don't think that still applies. You know, Prinzi, if I were a barkeeper, I'd give you a beer on the house for that. It's potentially brilliant, as you yourself would say."

"Oh, come on, don't try to con me. You can see Razaki is chuckling meaningfully. Why don't you simply ask for a free beer? Despite my better judgment, I think I'm in the mood to oblige."

"That's good to hear. So, let your action match your mood."

"To gods and cobwebs," Razaki toasted even as Prinzi fetched the drinks.

Prinzi turned around so quickly that the bottles nearly slipped out of his hands. "What did you just say, Razaki?" he asked. "Jesus Christ, that's quite a phrase. Nothing can save you now, my friend, from several barstool appearances in the great Maroko novel."

Both Ashikodi and Razaki exchanged knowing glances before they began to laugh.

"I've told you this before, Prinzi," Razaki said at last, "you're wasting your talents. You should be an actor."

And so it was that New Maroko woke up one morning to find copies of *Maroko Unlimited* being distributed free of charge. Its main report was headlined "Kaabiyesi Speaks," which immediately convoked a crowd around newsagents. According to the foreword, the report was a confession that Kaabiyesi had made to the paper in his factory-like house in Crocodile Island.

"My given name is Enamel, because my mother saw me as the son that will fetch the good things of life for her. I was born in my mother's half-room in a cheap brothel, at a time when my mother was already past her prime. I believe she used to charge less than the other women in order to get any customers at all. I often slept on the bare floor in her own partitioned half of the room, even on the infrequent occasions that she had customers. Inevitably, I saw more than I should have at that age. And I began to associate all adults, especially women, with the smell of coitus, especially the sort available in cheap brothels.

"One night, on one of the occasions I slept in my mother's bed, I could not help myself. I began to bounce up and down on top of her with frenzy. I was seven years old at the time. She threw me out.

"That was how I found myself homeless, a street urchin. I became a vagrant who would do anything for a meal. Perhaps in a bid to match the noble ancestry some of the other boys claimed for themselves, I presented myself as a prince fleeing from usurpers. Survival was the name of the game. I became anything and everything – porter, pickpocket, beggar, pimp. I was in and out of the remand home several times before the civil war broke out. I did not need to be conscripted. I volunteered.

"I was court-martialed just before the war ended and was lucky to get only a dismissal. Back on the streets, I joined a gang of burglars. Our first operation turned out disastrously. When I saw the man of the house on top of his wife, something in me exploded. Despite all the prior warnings by our leader, I cut the man quite cruelly with my matchet. The law soon caught up with me, after my gang members had expelled me. I was sentenced to fifteen years in prison.

"Inside, I worked my way up the hierarchy. It was at the Kirikiri Maximum Security Prison that I became 'Kaabiyesi,' a King Rat of sorts. Before I came out, I had started planning my next operation, solo this time.

"I think I had too much of a psychological hang-up to be a successful burglar. My victim this time was a rich widow. I raped her. I was nearly caught, so I fled to this island to escape justice. I have lived here, in hiding, ever since. I understand that the government has now issued a general amnesty for all war criminals, which curiously includes me. The widow was the wife of an army officer who was shot by a firing squad for his role in a botched coup attempt. In its way of thinking, the government classified her rape a war crime. It's incredible, but it doesn't really matter anymore.

"Here on the island, things have not gone very well for me. A crocodile went berserk one day and bit me. I now stand on the threshold of death and I have decided to make this confession to ease my conscience. Here, I have learned many hermit's truths and I do believe that all human beings will one day stand before the Judgement Throne of the Great Alone: I am that I am. I also make this confession because I understand that some persons are claiming to be my representatives and dressing me in divine robes. I am just a wretched fellow about to die and I have no interests worth representing. I am not interested in anything else but to make my peace with the Great Alone."

The publication created quite a tumult, with heated debates and sprinting speculations going on at almost every corner. Although Prinzi had a copy sent to Shanka that morning, the man made a great show of buying one. Dressed in a flowing white robe and with paid voices hailing him, he walked to the newsagent's in front of the Bonus Club, bought a copy of the paper, and returned home. Thereafter, he said or did nothing to acknowledge the report.

A reaction came in the form of a broadcast on Radio Kaabiyesi that evening. "I, Kaita Alhaji Kaita, the special agent of Kaabiyesi the Benevolent, have read the libelous concoction published in the so-called *Maroko Unlimited* on His Greater Excellency, Kaabiyesi the Benevolent. I wish to restate that Kaabiyesi is indeed the Prince of the Atlantic and is genuinely interested in the welfare of the people of New Maroko, his neighbors. In the fullness of time, Kaabiyesi will make a personal visit to New Maroko. I, therefore, call on the good people of New Maroko, my fellow residents, to pooh-pooh the so-called confession. Kaabiyesi forever!"

The next day, the police arrested Prinzi, whose name had appeared in *Maroko Unlimited* as the editor. The New Maroko

Development Board, led by a stern-faced Mrs Odukomaiya, evicted One from the bar. Segi had Prinzi's effects transferred to the Bonus Club for storage. She received a letter from the Development Board: "The Bonus Club is being put to a use for which no approval has been given. The Development Board is currently studying the development."

The tumult continued for some time.

"Wetin you think of this *Maroko Unlimited* matter?" Idi asked Orita.

"Ah, Shanka and Alhaji Kaita na better people-o. The two dey try for the poor of New Maroko. Shanka don help many people. Alhaji Kaita sef, e be like say the man dey do bazaar; na so im kindness plenty reach."

"So? Prinzi na bad man?"

"I no talk so. Prinzi get im own style, but the man no dey give credit at all at all."

"Look you! You no know say credit dey cripple business? Shanka sef be like say na some type of people na im e dey help, or else why e let Mama Badejo take frustration return to her village?"

"Wetin you dey talk, Idi? You know well well say Mama Badejo don make up her mind say she dey go, whether or whether not. Shanka sef na im give am the money to go, *abi* e for put the woman inside prison?"

"Well, me I no know who to believe. The two stories fantastic no be small, like say the Kaabiyesi na film actor. When I hear Shanka own that Christmas, when all those fancy cows and horse dey appear as if from ordinary air, me I believe am. When I read Prinzi them own, for black and white, I believe am too."

"Make we dey look now, as e be say Alhaji Kaita say the Kaabiyesi go come visit us."

"Na when be 'fullness of time'? Time dey ever full?"

"E be like say everything go full one day for this matter. Na for this kin' time I dey miss Ignatius and Goomsi well well."

"Abeg, no make me cry. This life!"

Quiet, who was asleep, began to snore. Orita shook him.

"Wake up, you tsetse fly man, before you go see Kaabiyesi for your sleep again. Wake up, yes, after all e be like say na you begin this *wahala*."

At the Bonus Club, Razaki, Ashikodi, and Segi sat conferring in Segi's bedroom – with Ray, One, and Linda sitting in.

"It's at a time like this that I sorely miss Madam Bonus," Segi lamented.

"Really, I don't think there's any insurmountable problem," said Razaki, "only that they're not allowing anyone to see Prinzi. We've tried, and One camps outside the police headquarters where he's being held."

"Poor Prinzi!"

"What? Don't let him hear you describe him like that."

"We should move his property and get a new place ready for him. Centigrade has agreed to rent two rooms in his new bungalow to Prinzi."

"Let's hope that they let Prinzi go and leave the matter at that."

"Is there any chance of that happening?"

"In this country, most things are matters of chance. You never know."

"You think the Development Board will allow Centigrade..."

"Since his isn't one of their houses, there isn't much they can do without provoking a major uproar. After reneging on their promise at the time they demolished Maroko, they'll probably let these shanties be."

"You know they wrote me a letter..."

"Oh yes, and that's not a good sign. But if they try to uproot the Bonus Club, they'll have to take on the whole of New Maroko as well."

"Thanks, Ashikodi, but there're too many forces at work here, what with Kaita and Shanka..."

"They must be up to something, unless they have money trees in their bedrooms. That Kaabiyesi Investments has a very small staff, mostly people pushing papers around, yet Kaita and Shanka are obviously getting richer every day. There's even believable talk that Kaita, despite appearances, doesn't live here at all but actually resides in New Queenstown – the old, dear Maroko. So, what is he doing here? Ordinarily, these shouldn't concern us much. But when they start stoking up a Kaabiyesi myth, which is linked to New Maroko, I begin to feel that the ground is being cut from under our feet once more."

When the meeting ended, Ashikodi did not leave immediately.

"Oh, go ahead, Razaki. I'm sure you can find your way past Odukomaiya's gate without me."

When he finally departed from the Bonus Club, Ashikodi walked on his head most of the way to the canoe that would take him to Coconut Island. He sang "Segi the Lola" in what some people said must have been a hundred voices.

Prinzi was released after two weeks. His reunion with One was unusually demonstrative. The two returned to New Maroko together.

A beaming Centigrade insisted on taking his tenant's temperature. "I think, Mr Prinzi, that you'll be around for a long time yet," he announced afterward.

"Good to hear, whatever it is worth. And thanks for the rental."

"It's a privilege, really, my pleasure. One is pleased at the opportunity of an experience different from the sort Mr World Bank provided."

Segi, Ashikodi, and Razaki soon arrived.

"The return of the saint!" said Ashikodi as soon as he stepped into the bar.

"*Aluta continua,*" Prinzi said with a clenched fist.

"Oh, Prinzi," said Segi, "what have they done to you? You've lost some weight, and One here is barely holding back more tears."

"*Aluta continua.*"

"You know, Prinzi," said Razaki, "your destiny may be stardom in the social action theater after all."

"*Aluta continua.*"

"Since when did this *aluta* start continuing, and with such monotony?" asked Ashikodi.

"It's the sign of the times. Do you know where I've been, man? I've been i-n-s-i-d-e! First, they sized me up with all sorts of questions: Who are the 'Unlimited' behind *Maroko Unlimited*? Did I know that our report on Kaabiyesi was capable of disrupting the peace here? Did I know that it is a major offense to publish an unregistered paper? And on and on, all these in a coffin-like room. And then they took me to a cell and locked me up. No visitors, no communication, nothing. For food, I had to force down a mess of porridge. That's where I've been, i-n-s-i-d-e!"

Centigrade reappeared bearing a food platter. "My modest contribution, Mr Prinzi, to your rapid recovery. Food has medi...cinal properties."

"This isn't modest at all, my friend, especially under the circumstances," Prinzi said as he began to eat. "As for the properties of food, I think that you understate the case."

"My sympathies, Prinzi," Segi said. "Only animals would treat a man in the manner you've described, perhaps in a bid to reduce him to their level."

"What do you expect from animals in power?" Ashikodi asked. "But we have to go on. The Communion of the Long Tide comes up soon in Coconut Island. I plan to invite the whole of New Maroko and to show them the ancestral home of Kaabiyesi's discredited father. I don't have to tell you that I may have to invent the evidence."

"And what will libation be without wine?" quoted Prinzi. "One, please do the honors."

One fetched drinks for everyone.

"What do you think of Ashikodi's idea, Prinzi?" Razaki asked.

"You know, when I was inside, I heard several voices, each

telling me what I should have or should not have done. And I realized anew that every battle is personal. This is our battle, my battle – even more so after my detention."

"I want to propose a toast," said Segi. "To Prinzi, to New Maroko, to Coconut Island, to the world inside and outside: peace!"

Peace was the mood occasioned in the settlement by talks about the Communion of the Long Tide. The Communion was the main festival in Coconut Island, which its inhabitants often adulated as "the Original Eden." Instead of an Original Sin, they spoke of an Original Pleasure. Both because of the sensual nature of the celebration and its magnificent cultural displays, it was quite popular. As the event approached, therefore, the atmosphere of blissful anticipation was palpable in New Maroko. Some of the residents had yet to visit Coconut Island and they eagerly looked forward to the experience, what with ringing tales about the wantonness of the women of the Original Eden during the Communion.

When the story also went abroad that the celebration that year would incorporate a visit to the ancestral home of Kaabiyesi's father, the mood began to change. Many people watched Shanka's goings and comings for ominous signs, but the man went about his business as if oblivious of the situation.

Three days to the festival, a band of fire-eaters and dancers led by Ashikodi dressed like an Asante warrior came to New Maroko to formally invite its residents to Coconut Island. Their performance, in front of the Bonus Club, drew a large crowd. The show was however soon overtaken by a small aircraft that appeared as if from nowhere and began a series of stunts at the other end of the settlement. The crowd promptly shifted its attention. As if in response to the dominant question below, the pilot wrote a name across the sky: Kaabiyesi! The crowd was fascinated by this instance of skywriting. The pilot then began to shower the crowd with currency notes. When the plane departed and after the scramble for the currency notes had ceased, the crowd began to sing an affirmation popularized by Pastor David:

> Me, I no go suffer
> I no go get problem
> God of miracles
> Na my papa-o
> Alpha and Omega
> Na my papa-o!

Although the pilot had barely been visible, he was portrayed by many of those who witnessed the appearance as an incandescent Kaabiyesi on an aerial survey of New Maroko.

"Na wa-o, that Kaabiyesi no be ordinary person at all at all."

"So, na true Shanka talk?"

That evening, Radio Kaabiyesi ran a broadcast by Shanka, preceded by an incantatory anthem that mentioned Kaabiyesi's name seven times.

"On behalf of Kaita Alhaji Kaita, I Alhaji Shanka El Shanka hereby invite the good people of New Maroko to a gala at the Palace of Good. The event, which will take place in three days' time, is to announce, two years in advance, the centennial of Kaabiyesi's current sojourn on earth."

Shanka an *alhaji*? Rumors that he had attended a School for Princes while on an extended pilgrimage to the Holy Land sprouted.

The visitors from Coconut Island, exhausted both from the scramble and from their unsuccessful attempts to interest the crowd in their performance once more, finally took their leave. In the same manner as their island was the first place God created, they said, Kaabiyesi was perhaps the second mystery.

"All numerals eventually connect with zero," said Ashikodi. "Nought is the void from which all things spring and the void to which all things return."

"I and I is truth," Haile greeted him when he encountered him that evening and increased his steps.

"What kind of truth?" Ashikodi shouted after him.

Three days later, the fleet of canoes that went to New

Maroko to ferry the residents to Coconut Island for the Communion of the Long Tide returned almost empty. Kaita's gala had triumphed.

A row of colorful booths outside Kaita's mansion enticed New Maroko residents with steaming delicacies and "games of chance" in which all players were winners. Praise singers and hornblowers swarmed around a pavilion where Kaita, Shanka, and Haile sat.

The main event was the arrival of three riderless horses, each bearing a card around its neck: "To the people of New Maroko, greetings – Kaabiyesi." As the horses came to a halt before him, Kaita prostrated. Almost everyone present followed his example. Shortly afterward, the guns began to boom – a ninety-eight-gun salute that kept many people on the ground for some time.

In Coconut Island, the Communion of the Long Tide progressed nevertheless – until the itinerant nature of the celebration brought the celebrants to the dilapidated hut soon identified as Kaabiyesi's ancestral home.

The hut was situated in the place where bonding sacrifices to the ocean were normally left. The consequent interpretation was that Kaabiyesi's ancestors were self-bonded slaves, not princes, of the Atlantic.

"Na im be say this Kaabiyesi na ordinary water servant e be."

"This world sef, na im e dey do big man say im be Prince of Atlantic!"

From the cracks in the walls of the hut, a white cage was visible to the crowd. The singing and dancing stopped. Puzzled, Ashikodi used a pole to prise open the lid. Several white pigeons emerged from the cage and flew into the air in a manner that clearly spelt K. Ashikodi, dressed like a town crier; Segi, like a princess; Razaki, like a drummer; Prinzi, like an Nri priest, were astonished.

Kaabiyesi?! Both a question and an exclamation.

Eleven

In the weeks that followed the Communion of the Long Tide, Ashikodi was not seen in New Maroko. When the residents of Coconut Island who normally came to New Maroko for various reasons reported his absence from his home, people began to speak of his "flight with the wind."

His return coincided with the reappearance of Maina, whose dismissal had been announced over the radio earlier that day. "Due to irreconcilable differences, His Excellency, Colonel Raji Omo-ale, the Governor of Lagos, has ordered the removal of Mr Maina Megida as the editor of *The Echo* with immediate effect."

Razaki had gone to Prinzi's Café on hearing the news. He was still there when Maina, elegantly dressed, walked in.

Prinzi glared at him before he sneered: "So, they sack you and the first place you could think of presenting yourself is my café. Well, *Mr* Megida, you're still persona non grata here."

Maina ignored him and sat beside Razaki on a barstool.

"Mr Prinzi," said Centigrade, who was also present, "I must point out that to my trained eye Mr Maina here is obviously ag...grieved. Under the circumstances, sympathy can be thera...peutic."

"Congratulations, Maina," said Razaki.

"Meaning?" queried Maina.

"Congratulations on your liberation from echoing nonsense. I see that you're in a celebratory mood yourself."

"I was attending a convention when I heard the news. Both the manner and the timing of the announcement were meant to ridicule me."

"What happened, Mr Maina? 'Irreconcilable differences' isn't fact-specific enough to enlighten medically minded gentlemen like me."

"The more obscure the charge the less its substance," said Maina. "The 'irreconcilable difference' has to do with a picture of the First Lady at one rural something or the other program that we published a few days ago. The governor complained that the picture didn't reflect her radiance and hinted that the First Lady was unlikely to be pleased. He must have been directed to remove me. Well, I still insist that the picture matched the story."

"And you've to come to my café to insist?" sneered Prinzi.

"I'm beginning to truly realize the capriciousness of these people."

"Hurrah!" exclaimed Razaki and Centigrade.

"You mean you're actually taking this Maina seriously?" Prinzi asked them. "I know his type. He's just lost out in the power game. Oh, he'll recover and then he'll be talking from the other side of his mouth."

"Listen to me, Prinzi..." began Maina.

"Really? You think that your dismissal has made me lose my mind?"

"What have I ever done to you, Prinzi, to deserve this hostility?"

"I'm not fond of people like you."

"This isn't kind at all. I came here to find some sort of understanding."

"Welcome, pilgrim. You're like a man with a terminal disease who goes to the cemetery to find a cure."

"Mr Prinzi," intervened Centigrade, "concerning Mr Maina here, I'm of the opinion..."

"Why don't you simply take the fugitive into your little clinic and let us be?" Prinzi cut him short.

Centigrade excused himself to attend to "urgent medical matters" and left.

"It's un-African to rejoice because of another fellow's misfortune. I hope you know the proverb that says 'Ask not whose corpse is being borne to the graveyard; it's also yours.'"

"I don't know any such proverb, Mr Maina, and I suspect you've just plagiarized John Donne's 'Ask not for whom the bell tolls...' Yours is the tribe sworn to plunder our gates of light, and it's a tribe that also feeds on itself. You fail to appreciate the logic of the echo. It gobbles sounds greedily, then vomits them compulsively. What then will the echo be without its greed?"

"To the people of New Maroko: greetings. To the denizens of Prinzi's Café: peace."

All eyes turned to the door, from where the salutations had come. Ashikodi stood there beaming.

"The 'Roko!" exclaimed Prinzi.

"'Kodi!"

"The event himself!"

The noise attracted One from the backroom. She embraced Ashikodi and bantered with him briefly before she left to attend to her cooking.

"Talk of homecoming!" Ashikodi said as he came into the bar. Prinzi offered him a beer.

Ashikodi turned to Maina. "Hello, Maina, I hear you've been promoted out of *The Echo* with an undisclosed price on your head."

"You heard? Where?"

"He's asking a question, people of the bar. Well, the wind told me that – and many other tales. Now, a toast before I translate this beer. To the people of New Maroko: abundance!"

They clinked glasses. Prinzi, who was not drinking, used his fist instead.

"So, where have you been, my friend?" he asked Ashikodi.

"We've been worried about you," Razaki added. "And 'we' includes Segi."

"The eye of sunlight! Well, the wind knocked on my door. It said: 'Come.' And I, Ashikodi, son of the wind, I followed my spirit, and we went through seven hills and seven valleys…"

"Hey, what's this? A folktale? This is Prinzi's Café, you know."

"In that case, I'll give you a simplified version: I took a vacation."

"You did?" asked Prinzi and Razaki.

"From what?" wondered Maina.

"From their questions you'll know them. After Shankaitakaabiyesi's triumph at the Communion of the Long Tide, I was fit to climb a tree, and a very tall one at that. I realized afresh that they're playing a game of destinations. But I, Ashikodi, I was born for the road, not for destinations. The journey that most people make in life is from romance to reality, so called. I've chosen instead to travel from romance to romance, the romance of the there and then to the romance of the here and now. Where the romance ends is where death begins, with its creepy certitude."

"Perhaps a poet," said Prinzi, "but what sort of story is that?"

"All right, I decided to take off and clear my head and to see the country once more. Sorry I didn't tell you, but I had actually departed before I properly knew what I was doing. I simply took a train and moved from place to place until I came back to where I departed from. I had a memorable time whistling with the wind, stopping by a village to share with the people the ear of an elephant or the hind of a goat, plucking banana damozels off the trees of coyness. Across the vast expanse of this country, I could clearly see once more the movement of Nigerian history. Land is still at the center of our conflicts."

"Land?"

"Yes, land, its resources. Where the land doesn't have any, those in power grab it anyway and carve it up for profit markets. That's what happened to Maroko."

"Did you have to take a trip, by train, to come to this conclusion?" asked Maina. "If you had been reading your newspapers..."

"How could I when people like you made newspapers unreadable? Anyway, mine was also a voyage from myself into myself."

"And now?" asked Razaki.

"I'll gather the people and tell them tales the wind told me."

"Ashikodi's parable of the road, I see-e," Maina said

scornfully.

"I wish I did."

"Oh, it's not that difficult, once you give it some thought. Ashikodi just had a holiday and unwound – plenty of wine, tumbles in the hay or wherever, and all that – and he's so full of the experience that his ventriloquism has become boundless."

A few days later, many New Maroko residents gathered outside Devil's Island on Sunday evening to hear Ashikodi's promised "Tales the Wind Told Me."

"My friends," Ashikodi began, "the wind said to me: 'Demonize the demonologists.' And that's why we've gathered here, not outside the Bonus Club. After the Communion of the Long Tide, the wind knocked on my door, and it said: 'Come.' I, Ashikodi, I'm the son of the wind. So, I followed it. It wasn't a hard decision to make. I have known many departures and arrivals, for I was born in a traveling circus.

"I was born on a day the wind went wild and danced the conga around the circus tents, so my parents named me Ikuku. The seers prophesied that my destiny would be like the dance of the wind. So, I became Ashikodi.

"My education began early. I don't mean being schooled in rhetoric, arithmetic, or writing. That came later. As a member of a traveling circus, I learned my geography quite early – about the living sand, the roaming road, the music of the earth, the nexus of fringe towns. I learned how to project appearance as reality. At ten, I had already mastered the skills of fire eating, ventriloquism, and headwalking. Appearance is reality.

"Oh, the circus was an open school of thrills. But the wind had other plans for me. A tempest buried our camp one night. The few survivors, excluding my parents, were rather confused and rudderless. The Nomadic Education Project swept me up, and my life turned a new chapter.

"I, Ashikodi, son of the wind, I'm the product of these two traditions. And that was how I became a poet. The wind, you see, is the poetry of life in motion. At school, I was mainly interested in studying the lives of great people – those who try to make the world brighter and better.

"My parents had moved from one camp to the other by following the wind and the stars. The wind taught me about indefinable things. My poetry is a search, through definable and indefinable passages, for the Great Indefinable. It isn't the poetry only of words. I've sometimes performed poems with my legs in the air. The world itself is like a mask dancing topsy-turvy. 'I scatter the leaves so that they will dance,' the wind told me.

"So, when the voice said 'come,' I didn't hesitate. I followed the voice. And it led me to the desert – through outposts of the spirit. We traveled behind the dung of camels through a vast wilderness in which I was a vanishing dot of dust. Our destination was the heart of the desert, an oasis. And the road said to me: 'This oasis was once a junction. All roads converged here, and so did all kinds of wayfarers. It soon became a thriving tent town. The first man to arrive named himself after the junction: Iyaka. Because he was the first to arrive and because he had named himself after the junction, Iyaka translated himself into an imperial majesty before whom everyone had to bow and tremble. He became both the body and the spirit of Iyaka. The other settlers watched his carryings-on with alarm, but his myth of origin and his rites of being swayed them.

"As the town prospered, so did Iyaka's imperial command. Then one morning Iyaka discovered that he was alone once more. The others had moved away, and they had dug a moat around what was once a junction town. Iyaka knew that he had entered his period of decline, and he gnashed his teeth. The earth had never liked the water all around, but it had been rendered powerless because it harbored the imperial Iyaka. So, the water began to devour the earth. Extinction stared the earth in the face, grinning with white teeth. The earth consulted its shrine of greatness, summoned its reservoir of strength and flung Iyaka to his perdition. Then it drove the water back with great bites of sand. But because it had once been a junction town and dreaded loneliness, it left an oasis.

"The people never came back, so the land grew into a vast wilderness. Yet this place had once been the kingdom of His Imperial Majesty, Iyaka, Son of the Earth. This place, which had once been a junction town, had also once upon a time been the center of a flourishing civilization. And it had been known as Kanemi, the ancestral kingdom of El Kaita, the patriarch. So the wind told me. And I remembered Maroko. I wrote my name, our names, on the pages of the water and the air. I, Ashikodi, I invoked the fire of the earth:

>   now heaves the famished road
>   and dust-coats undress ancient myths
>   gone, the cowering days
>   in palm frond cubicles
>   now, the people have carved the eve:
>   'rivers will urinate on the plumed heads
>   of the mountains
>   fires will vent their rage
>   on the pedicured throne
>   we neither seek crocodiles' skins
>   nor eagles' feathers
>   but neither can falter us now
>   now that the mask goes before
>   we shall spit
>   into the eyes of His Excellency'
>
>   yes, the people will renew their masks
>   again and again
>   yes, the people will erupt
>   from their palm frond cubicles
>   again and again
>   forever is the destiny
>   of palm frond masks

"Did anyone hear me over here?" The question was drowned out by the applause that greeted his rendition. The people crowded around him and chanted his praise names.

"Well, congratulations, you little tortoise," Prinzi said to him afterwards. "I was certain the people were going to burst your head for leading them on, but you managed to wriggle out of damnation in time."

"It seems you took off to rehearse the Song of Ashikodi," said Razaki.

"'By their compliments you shall know them.' So the road told me."

"Hey! This is not Devil's Island. This is Prinzi's Café, remember?"

Segi entered then.

"Hurrah!" shouted Ashikodi, almost falling down as he jumped off the barstool and hurried to hug her.

"At Devil's Island, the crowd kept us apart," he said to her. "And before I knew what was happening, these two dragged me away. All the time, I've been thinking of you."

"Is that the epilogue to tales the wind told you?" asked Segi. "You're having fun, aren't you, feeding the people with fables from ghost winds?"

"Jesus and Mary combined!" exclaimed Prinzi. "Say that again, slowly."

"When are you gentlemen going to visit Kaabiyesi Island, instead of wandering off and returning with tales about junctions and oases?" Segi demanded, ignoring Prinzi's request.

"But the whole of New Maroko knows we've already attempted such a visit," protested Razaki. He was referring to a trip the three made after the mysterious appearance of cows from the direction of Kaabiyesi Island.

"That was geography," replied Segi. "You came back to report that you circled the island three times and noted that it's smaller than New Maroko. Surely, we can see that ourselves. So too the barbed wire fence, which some people say can electrocute any intruder, the factory-like house, and the bright lights at night. As for the stone sculptures of crocodiles, the luminous 'Crocodiles on

Guard' notice, and the disembodied noises, who knows if your senses were affected by your fright? Anyway, all that is geography to me. I am talking about going there and requesting to see Kaabiyesi, whatever or whoever he is."

"Who will arrange such a visit?" wondered Razaki.

"I'm not talking about an arranged visit."

"You prefer breaking and entering?"

"When did the great Prinzi start speaking like a police summons?" said Ashikodi.

"I smell blackmail. I'll have you know that Prinzi is ever able."

"And you, Razaki?"

"Curtains up!"

"A drink on me!" said Segi excitedly.

"Why don't we invite Haile along?" Razaki said while Prinzi fetched the drinks.

"Some sort of insurance, eh? Not likely. Who but perhaps Shankaita can invite Haile to anywhere or anything these days? The old Haile has vanished."

So did the new Haile too. That night, the Rastafarian announced on Radio Kaabiyesi: "Good evening, New Maroko. This will be my last broadcast to you for some time. I'm going on my sabbatical. It's with great pleasure that I present to you tonight my brother in the house, DJ Oris the Dazzle, who will keep this station going in my absence. So, stay tuned to Radio Kaabiyesi. And remain blessed. Jah is."

Haile's disappearance became the focus of conversation at the Good Evening Hotel.

"Na true they talk say Haile man don vanish?" one of the girls asked Caro, Haile's girlfriend.

"Your mama!" Caro said menacingly.

"And your papa! Why you dey abuse me because I ask you the thing wey I hear about your boyfriend?"

"Which kin' talk be that say Haile the man don vanish? Na you vanish am? No be Haile come here day yesterday?"

"E no tell you anything, because na that yesterday they say e announce for Radio Kaabiyesi say e dey go 'abbatical.'"

"Where be that? Come, if na play make you stop am-o! Maybe na you don dey spread the 'tory for town."

"This one wey you dey do sef, maybe two of una don plan am, like Shanka and Epi Eye."

"Which one be this now, Rachel? Small time, person go begin think say na true you dey talk."

"Come, you still dey this Maroko sef, *abi* you go Egypt?"

When Caro finally confirmed that Haile had, indeed, announced that he was going on "abbatical," the fight drained out of her.

"My sister, *ashawo* no be work," she said sadly. "Na bastard comma."

"Maybe e don waka like Shanka. That means say when e come back e fit rich like Shanka too."

"Shanka rich, you see am for Epi Eye body?"

"Look you! You never hear say Epi Eye don get better boutique for Cotonou?"

"True?"

"Na so I hear-o."

"God dey. Ah, Haile the man!"

Twelve

Although their second trip to Kaabiyesi Island was made in broad daylight, the trio of Prinzi, Ashikodi, and Razaki came back without accomplishing their mission. Segi had organized a reception. The girls from the Bonus Club sang and danced around the three men as they came ashore, fluttering white handkerchiefs and decorating them with garlands. Ashikodi did a few dance steps, but he was as upset as Prinzi and Razaki. If Segi noticed, and they could have sworn that she did, she paid no heed. The singing and dancing continued – until Ashikodi held up his hand.

"Our people," he said. "We have been to Kaabiyesi Island. But we did not see Kaabiyesi. Instead, we saw Haile."

"Haile?"

"Yes, Haile. We disembarked in front of what must be the main gate – a massive stone sculpture of a crocodile. Nothing happened. So, we began calling out. 'Hello!' 'Hallo!' 'Anybody here?' We called out until our voices were becoming hoarse. Suddenly, Haile appeared as if from nowhere. He must have had a haircut because the dreadlocks were gone, and he looked strange in a double-breasted suit. Before we could tease him about his appearance, he held up his right hand. 'Speak to the hand,' he said. Speak to the hand? Anyway, we stated our mission: we had come to call on Kaabiyesi.

"'Such beautiful people are never forgotten,' he said.

"A strange response, you will agree. 'Cut it out,' said Prinzi. "We said we're here to call on Kaabiyesi. Since you've become a gateman, please announce us.'

"His response this time was even stranger. He began to chant a nursery rhyme:

'Thirty days hath September
April, June, and November
All the rest have thirty-one
Except February alone'

"When he finished, he declared that Kaabiyesi did not have us in his appointment book that day and that his appointment book was already filled for the next one year.

"'Haile, this is not a joke,' entreated Razaki.

"Gentlemen, this is Kaabiyesi Island, not a joke factory,' he said. 'Come back next year and, God willing, Kaabiyesi will see you.'

"'Are you sure there is a Kaabiyesi at all? Have you seen him yourself?' I demanded.

"'Does God exist?' he retorted. 'And have you seen Him yourself? Now, that will be all, gentlemen. Good day.'

"Of course, we protested. He merely regarded us, then he raised his left hand. Pandemonium. A volley of vultures appeared from the bowels of the island on a homicidal mission. And we ran for our dear lives."

Prinzi later hatched the plan of having Idi report to the police that illegal mining was going on at Kaabiyesi Island. His plan was to have the police swoop down on the place and, in the process, expose whatever was going on there. Instead, Idi returned to New Maroko battered and bruised.

When Idi went to the police station, the desk sergeant listened to him without a word. After he had stated his complaint, the sergeant asked him a plethora of questions.

"Name?"
"Age?"
"Sex?"
"Place of origin?"
"Present address?"
"Marital status?"
"Number of children?"
"Name of spouse?"
"Occupation?"
"Height?"
"Weight?"
"Chest measurement?"

"Religion?"
"Next of kin?"
"Any police record?"
"Any facial marks?"
"Annual income?"
"Nationality?"
"Permanent address?"
"Educational status?"

The sergeant then asked an alarmed Idi to wait. When he returned, he led the man to the office of the Divisional Police Officer. Idi had to answer the same questions, and more, all over again.

"You from Maroko," declared the DPO finally, "you want us to raid the Island of the Blessed? It's on record that many people perished during the demolition of Maroko. How are we sure you're not one of those people?"

Idi said he was obviously not.

"Shut up! You must be a zombie. As such, you have no status under the law."

Idi's worry at that point was not his status under the law. He was concerned with restating that he was certainly alive and well. The police officer asked his men to "deal with him." And they beat him cruelly – as if they wanted to transform him into a zombie.

Centigrade, who had taken to nursing Idi in the battered man's residence, was nonplussed. "But how could this happen?" he asked no one in particular. "This is similar to what happened to me the other time. They encouraged some of my fellow detainees to put horns on my head, not that I ever complained about my phy...sique."

"My God go answer them with fire," fumed Iya Idi.

Both Orita and Quiet, who converged at their usual spot at night, were astonished.

"This world don spoil finish," said Orita. "How the police go batter Idi Baba like that because e go report say Kaabiyesi dey do *jibiti* for yonder?"

"The police na your friend," said Quiet, echoing a radio jingle.

"True, for radio. But how Idi sef come 'gree go that kin' message for Prinzi them? Their own legs bend?"

"Ah, you know say all of them don get police number. Like say they take their own legs reach that police station, the police for disappear them one time."

"Anyway, for Devil's Island, them dey complain say Idi Baba never come work for three days now. Even sef, them dey talk say they wan' sack am. You don hear that kin' thing before?"

"They never hear wetin happen?"

"Iya Idi take her mouth come report, still they no wan' hear. We don already talk am say we no go 'gree. The devils for Devil's Island don too plenty sef, they still wan' carry another one join. We no be zombie, we no go 'gree."

The words formed the protest song of the incensed workers at the incinerator the next day:

> We no be zombie
> We no be zombie
> We no go 'gree

The workers were on strike. Their grouse was the dismissal of Idi for being absent from work for four days without prior permission. Beyond that immediate cause, they were also protesting their poor working conditions.

The management responded by hiring new workers. The striking workers barred their entrance. The management invited the New Maroko Development Board. Although the dreaded Mrs Odukomaiya threatened the striking workers with eviction from the settlement, they would not budge; they jeered at her instead. The management then called in the police, guns and all. The workers remained steadfast.

Shanka intervened. He got the police to withdraw. And he negotiated with the management, ensuring that all the workers – including Idi – were reinstated. Then he spoke with the workers, promising them better working conditions. "Listen to me, people," he appealed. "I, Shanka El Shanka, you know that when I say something will be done, it is done. Go back to work. New Maroko needs your services."

The workers called off the strike and returned to work. The next day, a report about the strike appeared in *The Echo*. It was headlined "New Maroko Patriot Quells Strike at the Incinerator." The report carried a full-length picture of Shanka and mentioned his name sixteen times.

At Prinzi's Café, the strike was the main subject.

"You should have settled the dispute and received all the media attention, not Shanka," Ashikodi said to Prinzi.

"If I had tried to do that, there would probably have been a case of accidental discharge from those police guns."

"So, what was it you did about Idi? If I remember correctly, you were the one who sent him to that accursed police station."

"Would you rather have gone there? And would that have achieved a better result? I paid Idi's medical bill, as you know. But, more importantly, Idi is not one to undertake a mission he doesn't believe in. Whatever he did he did for New Maroko."

"Anyway, it's remarkable that the police would not listen to Idi but they did Shanka's bidding with a snap of his fingers. You see, that is the whole point: justice should be one; it should not be divisible."

"Justice is one. It is indivisible," Prinzi said slowly, his face aglow. "The 'Roko himself! You must have been born on the day the spirits infused the power of speech into man. Nothing can save you now..."

"May I come in?"

A young woman stood at the entrance.

"Depends on who or what you are," said Prinzi, "although this is a café – the best in New Maroko."

"I am a reporter for *The Echo*."

"Are you in any way related to a certain report about a so-called New Maroko patriot?" Prinzi asked.

"Yes, I am. My name is Efe Williams."

The reporter came forward and offered her hand. Prinzi ignored her. Ashikodi shook his head but accepted the handshake.

"In that case, I must warn you that I've taken the precaution of acquiring a bucket of disinfectant," Prinzi said to the reporter. "For echoes like you. How do you want it – before or after?"

"Prinzi! The latitude to be, remember? Let's hear her out."

"Depends on what she has to say."

"Look, the report that was published was quite different from what I wrote."

"Incredible! You mean you came here to tell tales? Is it not obvious to you that here is New Maroko and that this place is Prinzi's Café?"

"Look, these things happen. Even stranger things take place. Let me tell you the story of Kabuki. He was one of the best in our newsroom, meticulous and conscientious. His reports were also routinely re-angled. Kabuki wasn't one to let such things happen without an uproar. Strange things began to happen to him. One night, he was working on a story about the release of some environmental rights activists. Then he heard on the Network News that some of them had been rearrested. You know the Network News. The Ministry of Information more or less approves every broadcast. So, Kabuki put the bit about the rearrest in his story. The next day, he received a query. No such item had been broadcast. He was stupefied, but he recovered quickly. Next, he was working on a story about a novelty football match between army officers' wives and police officers' wives. He heard on the Network News that the football association had overturned the result in favor of army officers' wives. He included that in his story. Again, no such item had been broadcast. He was suspended.

"When he returned to the newsroom, Kabuki took to recording the Network News. When he heard it broadcast that Colonel Omo-ale had agreed to workers' demand for increased wages, he wrote the story. The editor was waiting for him. The story was never published, and Kabuki was fired. He tendered his tape. Guess what was on it? A report about a plane crash in

Ouagadougou."

"Either you or your Kabuki must be quite a storyteller," said Prinzi. "What are you still doing in your crummy newsroom?"

"I believe her," said Ashikodi. "I'm inclined to. Some stories are too strange to be fiction."

"Like Kaabiyesi?"

"That's another matter altogether. There's some sort of sleazy motive in that. Why would this young woman venture here now to lie to us?"

"She could be a spy."

"Look," said Efe, "cross my heart, nothing I have told you is untrue. Like Kabuki, I started working for *The Echo* because I needed a job. Now, I've been commissioned to write for an international wire service. That's why I'm here. I'm interested in New Maroko. On the face of it, there's nothing but squalor here and an obvious case of environmental degradation – what with the incinerator, the pollution of the ocean finger, and man-made islands. I've done some research. The land belongs to Kaabiyesi Investments. The land certificate was signed by the governor not too long before Maroko was demolished."

"Kaabiyesi Investments, not Kaabiyesi or Kaita?"

"What's the difference? Kaabiyesi owns a majority of the shares. The company received payment for land lease; there was no outright sale. If you clean up the ocean finger and take into account the land area as well as proximity to downtown Lagos, this place is prime real estate."

"Welcome to the café, my friend," said Prinzi, offering the reporter a seat and a drink.

"The Seven Fingers may yet be complete again," Ashikodi said to Prinzi. To Efe, he said: "It means that Kaabiyesi Island was developed around the time that monkey, Omo-ale, signed the land certificate. None of us has ever seen Kaabiyesi."

"There's probably a Kaabiyesi. But after learning of your experience, I've made no attempt to seek him out. I don't want to be obvious. There are parcel bombs, coup plot charges, and imprisonment to beware of in this country."

"Is Colonel Omo-ale a shareholder in Kaabiyesi Investments? Do you know?"

"I hope to find out. I only pray an epidemic doesn't wipe out this place before then. That was actually my original story: 'Incinerator Strike Forewarns of an Epidemic?'"

Her fear was prophetic. An epidemic soon broke out in New Maroko. The immediate cause was not known, but there were many fingerposts – the incinerator, with its "fumes of poison"; the festering gutters, with their fat and mean mosquitoes; the putrid abattoir, with its convocation of malevolent vultures and freak rats. There was even a scare, suspected to have been originated by the girls at the Good Evening Hotel, that their competitors at the Bonus Club had infected the men with a sexually transmitted Acquired Immune Deficiency Syndrome. New Maroko woke up with a shudder. Some of the residents went about coughing like backfiring engines. They counted themselves lucky. Kaita, the story spread, fled abroad. Wearing a handkerchief over his face, Shanka appeared at the Bonus square to counter the story. Kaita, he said, had gone in search of a solution.

On Radio Kaabiyesi, DJ Oris the Dazzle played his favorite musical composition, "Children of Paradise," over and over again. "People of the kingdom," he said in his lilting voice, "this is a season of trial. But it will pass. We have the venerable Kaita Alhaji Kaita's promise. So, do not grow weary in spirit. We're at the dawn of greatness. Great shall our trials be. Great too shall be our triumph. Peace and love!"

But there was no peace. And not much love. On the second day, the epidemic claimed its first victim. Quiet, who had insisted on dragging himself to his station even in his hollow condition, fell while he was waving his flag. The train rattled past.

His funeral, which Shanka quickly organized, witnessed the unusual – the absence of most New Maroko residents. Idi, who claimed his ordeal at the police station had made him immune to any epidemic, wept.

"Here was an old man," said Ashikodi, "but he could not grow old in peace." So far, the epidemic had not touched him because, he said, he mediated between the living and the spirits. But midway into the funeral, he began to cough and to feel dizzy. He promptly returned to Coconut Island, saying that the devil was on the loose in New Maroko.

Razaki came to the funeral wearing a mask. Prinzi, whose eyes had become as red as fire, attended wearing dark goggles, which Razaki said made him look like the Medusa.

"Better the Medusa than a masquerade," he snapped.

Orita tried to attend, but he collapsed on his doorstep and had to crawl back to bed. Segi, who coughed as if there were nails in her gullet, sang a farewell song from her window; thereafter, she led a prayer session for the dead man in the shuttered confines of the Bonus Club.

New Maroko shut down.

Centigrade, who secretly thanked God the epidemic had not disgraced him, became a darling everywhere with his effusive sympathies and "power drugs." In his heart, he began to make plans to build another house. He had already built two. Ray received a "special calling." He quit the Bonus Club and became "a worker in the Lord's vineyard of miracles." He founded a mobile ministry that he called Ray of Hope and went about singing and dancing:

> Abraham's blessings are mine
> Abraham's blessings are mine
> I am blessed in the morning
> I am blessed in the evening
> Abraham's blessings are mine

He was full of blessings that season. He blessed the rich and the poor, the sick and the healthy, the earth and the ocean finger, the sinners and the saints. He chastised them too. "Did you think that because the Lord was awaiting your repentance He was asleep? Bless you, my people, but you have sinned and come short of the glory of God. And the wages of sin is death. But you shall not die. This is the special miracle that the Lord has promised through me.

But you have to help me to save you. There are special prayers to be said. There are special candles to be burned. But gold and silver have I not. What are you waiting for, O Maroko? Rise up and save yourselves. So says the Lord."

Wherever he received an offering, he made a mark on the door. "When He sees the sign, He shall pass over," he said.

The incinerator temporarily closed down. The Development Board declared a "rain recess" and shut its office. The finger-pointing became worse.

"Those cheap Good Evening girls are determined to put us out of business," Segi told her girls. Her cough had improved because of a concoction Madam Bonus had taught her how to make. "And that crook, Ray, they say that when he talks about the city of sin, he looks this way."

"Don't mind them. Na jealousy. Na we make New Maroko be like abattoir?" wondered Linda.

"That Ray self! Once a criminal always a criminal," said Joy.

"Anyway, he's not our problem anymore. I'm sure people will soon find out that he's a fraud and lynch him."

"Who get strength or spirit to lynch anyone in these times?"

"But how they go dey talk say na we bring AIDS enter New Maroko? Who see the AIDS? And Quiet wey die, everyone know say e no dey follow woman."

"My dear, people are not thinking straight right now. That's the worst thing about the epidemic. But, hopefully, it will pass soon. How is Charity today?"

"Strange. You should visit her again today, madam. E be like say she dey better each time when you go see am."

"Let's go and see her again. What sort of illness is this that will drain away her immense vitality?"

They found Charity, her vivacity and buxom appearance since gone, behaving strangely. Although there was no water in the room, she was making swimming motions on her bed as if swimming through a deep river. When some of the girls tried to hold her, she threw them off with astonishing energy. Segi told them to let her be. They began to pray for her instead. When she finally sank into her bed, she thrashed around for a while. And that was it.

Her death unexpectedly served to answer the allegations that she and her colleagues had brought a sexually transmitted terminal disease into New Maroko. The story that circulated was that she had been married to a river spirit in another world and he had finally taken her away from the known world.

Grief hung like smoke clouds over the Bonus Club. Questions too.

"Maybe Charity, God rest her soul, get this AIDS true true," Linda said to Segi. "Look how death dry am before e carry am go. What are we going to do now, all of us?"

"Already, those girls at the Good Evening Hotel are rejecting our regular customers. You want to help them?"

Nevertheless, she closed the Bonus Club for the time being and arranged for the girls to be tested for AIDS.

Kaita returned the day after Charity's burial with a truckload of medical personnel wearing tight gloves. They set to work immediately and managed to stop the epidemic. The incinerator opened its gate once more. The Development Board ignored the rain and hurried back. Kaita became "Kaita Alhaji Kaita the Magnificent," according to a description popularized by DJ Oris the Dazzle.

Centigrade, whose "power drugs" had been overtaken by events, only managed to paint his residence. Ray abandoned his "special calling" and scurried back to the Bonus Club. But no one called him Ray again. He became known either as Hope or Miracle.

"This time, Segi is setting a bad example," grumbled Prinzi, who had happily put away his dark goggles. "She shouldn't have taken that fickle fraud back."

"Mr Prinzi," said Centigrade, who was 'taking a break' at the bar. "Judgment is the Lord's."

"Go on, give me a chapter from religion, that eternal

opium. Just like Haile asking us whether God exists. Does God exist? Does He not? Meanwhile, people exploit His name to their own advantage."

"You now want to run both Prinzi's Café and the Bonus Club?" asked Razaki, who had also speedily put his mask away. "Well, after the epidemic, all things are possible."

"Em, gentlemen..." cut in Centigrade, "a terrible thing like that epidemic shouldn't be spoken about in such loud tones. It may still be lur...king around. Of course, I am com...pounding..."

"Better put some alcohol in whatever you're up to this time. The thing tasted like urine the last time, not that it worked."

"Oh no, Mr Prinzi..."

"You mean the great Prinzi has become one of Dr Swallow's patients? Signs and wonders!"

"Em, em, gentlemen..."

"In Prinzi's Café?" asked Ashikodi as he walked in, radiating good health. "In that case, the epidemic must have been Noah's Flood on a return sweep. Anyway, take a look at this."

He was referring to a syndicated report in a newspaper. Headlined "Environmental Abuse Unleashes Epidemic," it bore the byline of E. F. Smaili. The report attributed the epidemic to the "poisonous fumes" from the incinerator, but it also criticized the Development Board and New Maroko residents for poor hygiene. And it warned that the reckless transformation of a part of the ocean into Kaabiyesi Island was an open invitation to disaster.

"Hmm, not bad," Razaki said. "Who's this fellow, E. F. Smailli?"

"Sounds to me like Efe Williams scrambled," said Ashikodi. "I've been thinking about it."

"Hiding behind a village of invisible coconuts, I'm sure."

"Prinzi! Anyway, I'll see you later. I have a date with Segi."

"Congratulations, Mr Ashikodi. She is a very the...ra...peutic specimen."

"And how come you know so much, Dr Swallow?"

"Oh, I am immen...sely fond of the Bonus Club at night.

Who is not?"

"Well," said Razaki. "There's talk that there are strange things about the Bonus Club these days. No offense meant but..."

"Not to worry. You have offended already – and been pardoned."

"Are you visiting Segi or is she being visited by you?" Prinzi asked mischievously.

"I've heard it said that you would argue behind the leg of a donkey. Count me out today." He left, whistling "Segi the Lola."

"Love is like an epidemic, you know," said Prinzi. "It eats you up."

"Very memorably said," noted Razaki. "But how come you're still in one piece?"

"It eats each person up differently."

"Rather love then than the epidemic."

**Book 4
Kaita Beach**

Thirteen

The construction of the Anniversary Square had not been as fast as the people had expected, but the result was an impressive theme park ringed by stone sculptures of crocodiles. The contractor, a woman with a fondness for headgears that looked like pyramids, was rumored to be Shanka's girlfriend. The rumor was never confirmed, but it was Shanka who announced the date for the dedication of the square.

Kaita was billed to cut the tape as the Father of the Day. He arrived in a horse-drawn carriage preceded by hornblowers. After cutting the tape, to tumultuous applause, he declared he had a letter from Kaabiyesi.

"Children of the kingdom, I send you my sincere felicitations on the dedication of the square commemorating your exodus from Maroko. I am proud to be associated with this event through my representatives, Shanka El Shanka and Kaita Alhaji Kaita the Magnificent. It is my wish that the square be known as Shanka Square and that the area presently known as New Maroko be called Kaita Beach. Remain blessed."

The reading of the letter, punctuated by Kaita's hornblowers, was followed by the appearance of nine garlanded white cows, each one bearing an alphabet of Kaabiyesi's name: Kaabiyesi. Kaita informed the crowd that the cows were Kaabiyesi's gift to New Maroko in the spirit of the occasion. He then unveiled a sign that advertised the theme park as Shanka Square. Kaita Beach, he promised, would soon witness a beautification project that would transform a part of the waterfront to a beach resort.

Shanka spoke – about how proud he was to have the square named after him. The project, he said, was the first step toward the complete transformation of Kaita Beach. "My people," he said, "you are living in paradise, and you will yet know it."

Soon after the ceremony, a large notice that identified the entire area as Kaita Beach appeared on top of the entrance gate to the settlement. Stone sculptures of crocodiles environed the notice.

Work began on the waterfront, on what many New Maroko residents dubbed "Crocodile Resort." Supervised by the Development Board, the construction of roads in the settlement also began.

"Strange things are happening all around," Prinzi said to Razaki. "Very strange."

"That remarkable lady, Efe – a truly remarkable lady – was right. What's happening here is beginning to look like that infamous land use decree at work."

"But we go still dey here when they do all the shine shine?" asked Orita. He and Idi were on one of their infrequent visits to Prinzi's Café.

"My worry, exactly," said Prinzi. "A beach resort in New Maroko. Who among us can afford to pay a pound of flesh for a glass of red water and sugar?"

"Ah, Oga Prinzi, wetin be that?" asked Orita.

"Na 'Chapman' better people dey call that kin' drink," said Idi with the disdain of a former Shelling Hotel employee.

"Oh, I don forget say you been do boy-boy for that sniff-and-quench hotel," snapped Orita.

Both Prinzi and Razaki could not help laughing.

"I no blame you," Idi said to Orita. "How you no go forget? Na your kin' person them dey arrest for Shelling gate for attempted entry."

"Attempted entry?" said Prinzi. "Sounds to me like a good way of dealing with the Mainas of this world. Anyway, let them beautify the place. Why should we complain? No one is asking us to move, and God knows that this time we'll never move."

"I wish the 'Roko were here," said Razaki. "He must have something to say about these transformations."

"Except Segi the Lola, who sees the 'Roko these days?"

"Oga Prinzi," said Orita, "na true say Ashikodi wan' marry Segi?"

"Where did you hear that?"

"Na so I hear am-o. Them dey talk say the two wan' begin

do joint show for Bonus Club. Na true?"

"My friends, love can do all things."

"You know, that's a brilliant idea," said Razaki, "a duet by Segi and Ashikodi at the Bonus Club. That's what we need here to feel like the living. A toast to life – the Segi and Ashikodi project. I'm interested in it."

"You too wan' dance, Mr Razaki?" asked Idi.

"I'm sure he wouldn't want to task his little legs in that manner," said Prinzi, laughing. "He's probably going to be some sort of conductor."

"Inside Bonus Club? Na bus?"

"Oh no, not a bus conductor. You know, some kind of director."

"Prinzi!"

The call cut short Razaki's reply. It was One, who had been out, signaling Prinzi to the street door. A commotion in the street beckoned to the others.

The tumult marked the arrival of Opio, a snake charmer and stomach sawyer. A short, muscular man who walked with a swagger as if he owned the earth and all its secrets, he arrived in Kaita Beach like a parade. Behind him marched two drummers and a bag carrier. On his body were entwined ferocious-looking snakes. Opio appeared oblivious of the snakes. He marched like a soldier singing, in a booming voice, a war song:

>*Agabanam ikwa mgbo n'Uzuakoli*
>*Agabanam ikwa mgbo*
>*Nwa ada m n'ebe*
>*Si mgbo atukwala m n'obi-o*
>Baby, *isi m gbalaga?*
>*Onye g'akwa mgbo ma Hausa bia*
>Baby, *isi m gbalaga?*
>*Onye g'akwa mgbo ma Hausa bia*
>
>*Tamuno muno-e-e-e*
>*Tamuno muno*

Enemy plane *agbafe na*
Tamuno muno
Ojukwu nye m egbe ka m gbatuo ya
Tamuno muno

Opio was a traveling magician. In Kaita Beach, he held several performances at different locations. Shanka Square soon became his favorite spot. Before each performance, he would pass round a tin can. On a good day when the can was filled, he would take a long, sharp knife – he usually demonstrated its sharpness by casually slicing an object with a single thrust – and begin to saw his naked stomach, provoking disembodied squeaks but never any wound. On a bad day, he would merely position the snakes at different angles and demonstrate his ability to command them.

But whatever the nature of the day, whether good or bad in his reckoning, he talked about Biafra. He had been a soldier in Biafra during the war. Ojukwu, the Biafran leader, was his hero, and his beard had been groomed to resemble Ojukwu's own during the war.

Opio's excursion through history usually began with his singing one of his favorite songs:

> Take my bullet when I die
> O Biafra
> Take my bullet when I die
> O Biafra
> Take my bullet when I die
> Hallelujah
> If it happens tomorrow
> I die forever
> Biafra, take my bullet when I die

As he sang, he swaggered about among the poised snakes, usually concluding with a warrior dance. He became known as "Opio *Egwu*" or "Opio the Dance."

"Ah, we fight-o, no be small. We fight. The thing wey I do for Uzuakoli, the grass no go ever forget am. I use one bullet kill plenty plenty enemy soldiers. I come capture one; na im teach me this snake and stomach business. But they wound me-o. They wound me so-tey I bleed all the blood wey dey my body comot. That's why when I put knife for my stomach, blood no dey comot again.

"Wetin happen? We comot for our home scatter everywhere come be like people wey no get home again. Na im they begin kill us like fowl for the thing wey we no know, wey we no do. They even cut human head put inside train send to Ojukwu, take blood write for inside the train: 'This is for Ojukwu.' *Mba*, that one too much! If person no fit waka for this earth like person, better make they bury am inside. Biafra! Who no know know.

"But war terrible, no be small. For my village, e been get one man wey dey sell scent, so everyone dey call am St Lele. Our people like am well well, so when war start some people convince am make e no go back to im place, say e don become one of us. But when soldiers retreat reach our village, wetin happen? They seize St Lele, carry am go for market square, take pestle pound am like yam. The whole village scatter. 'Lele, Lele, you don die yet?' the soldiers go ask am. 'No, I never die,' e go mumble. They go begin pound am again – until e die finish. They take knife cut am up, share the meat for the whole village. Till today, they still dey talk about St Lele for my village. You see how war be?"

Orita tried to become his pupil, but Opio would only teach him how to swagger and dance. Kaita Beach appealed to him, so he decided to settle there for some time. "No be say person wan' stay here till e die, but person go rest small first." He camped beside Shanka Square, ignoring the Development Board's eviction notice. At night, he fraternized with the waterfront group. He taught them how to scent their marijuana. From time to time, he took his act out of Kaita Beach, sometimes staying away from the settlement for as long as a week. Both at the Bonus Club and the Good Evening Hotel, he became a familiar presence.

The next person to arrive was Chief Tanker, as he asked to be called. He was a tall, fat man with a twitching head and a potbelly that he rubbed with pride.

"I be drinker," he would say. "We wey drink Delta water as our mama milk, wetin be beer? You know Delta water? Na heavy *ogogoro* wey dey salute throat with fire."

After he heard the story of Maroko, he said his regret was not having met Madam Bonus. "E be like say man for like am no be small."

Like Opio, Chief Tanker took to socializing with the waterfront group at night. He preferred his bottle of dry gin to their marijuana, although he was an occasional smoker. He was also fond of Prinzi's Café and visited there whenever he could. "My brother," he would sometimes complain, "that Prinzi, e know all the book finish but credit no dey im dictionary."

"That man, the one with a pendulum for a head," Prinzi said about him, "he has quite an appetite, only his pocket is not as deep."

The newcomer had his own story to tell. "My original name na Oghenebiko: God, abeg! My main town na Jesse. Na there oil pipeline burst, catch fire, roast people like grasscutter. One thousand, one t-h-o-u-s-a-n-d people, even pass, die just like that. Still, they come dey speak grammar for our head say the people wey tap oil for burst pipe dey do illegal activity. My brother, how person go see oil dey leak e go just look am comot eye when the thing be like diamond? If person sell only one bucket, that one fit buy bag of rice. One t-h-o-u-s-a-n-d die for small village, still the world no shake. E just be like say na cockroach na them die inside pit latrine, eh? Na im I run comot."

He had lost almost his entire family in the disaster, and that was why, he said, he had taken to wearing a tortoise necklace and carrying a fly whisk.

"My mama, she been get tortoise farm for Jesse. No be anyhow tortoise-o, but correct ones wey everyone get im own name sef. When the evil happen, na only me and my sister remain. I leave the farm for am, carry my papa flywhisk enter road. This small tortoise wey I also carry, na the day wey the evil happen na im they born am. I come name am after my mama: Nyerhovwo."

His dream, he said, was to start his own tortoise farm one day.

Chief Tanker was in Kaita Beach as a new railwayman. At the request of the railway corporation, the Development Board allocated him the room Quiet had occupied.

"One thousand die for Jesse, na im e be like say you wan' take gin drown yourself," Opio said to him. "You know how many people die for Biafra? One m-i-l-l-i-o-n, m-o-r-e than one million!"

"One million plus die for war time, for thirty months; one thousand plus die for peace time, for one day. Wetin you think? Biafra sef, they don talk am so-tey God in heaven don hear. Jesse, e just be like smoke wey they never even see well for capital. But the oil wey them dey put for pipe carry go one thousand miles, na we own. How you see am?"

"I see am," Opio nodded, "but you know how many people wey gully swallow for my town, Nanka, in one day? You don hear the story before? Oh-ho!"

"Opio!" Idi cut in. "You no dey tire sef? This one carry snake come, this one carry tortoise; this one from Biafra, this one from Jesse. Na so Kaita Beach wan' be?"

"I wonder-o," murmured Orita.

"If you like, wake," said Opio. "How you go understand when e no happen to you? All this one wey una dey do for here, make una wait until Kaabiyesi hungry well well. I hear say na every hundred years na im e dey chop. Who you think chop the town wey been dey here before, *abi* why you think say that Kaita no allow epidemic kill all of una finish?"

"In short, I dey go home," protested Idi, but he made no move to leave. "Which one be this one now, you snake man, *abi* you wan give person hypertension? Orita, make you careful with this man-o!"

"Why you think say I dey give am water to bathe? Snake no dey bite person wey e know."

After Opio and Chief Tanker came Asampete, a stunning beauty with a soulful laugh. Her name, she told anyone who cared to know, meant "Dazzling Beauty" in Igbo.

"But I'm not Igbo. At least, I don't know whether I am. I don't even know what I am."

Her mother had been abandoned at birth and had grown up at an orphanage run by an Igbo woman. Later, she met and married a Yoruba teacher. Her husband eventually left her because she was seemingly barren. She knocked around for some years before she founded an orphanage herself. Along the line, she was involved in a brief romance with a traveling salesman who was secretive about his roots. It was after he had vanished that she discovered that she was pregnant. As her daughter, Asampete, grew, she developed the same urge as her mother: to discover her roots.

"You know how this ethnic porridge of a country is. It can be terrible not knowing where one truly belongs. So, I began to consult a well-respected psychic. And, better believe it, I began to see my father in my dreams. Then, recently, I saw his picture in the newspaper – as one of the victims of the New Maroko epidemic. And here I am. Finally, I have a father, roots!"

Quiet!

From Idi and Orita she learned that Quiet had spent several years in jail. They also had stories to tell, from what the man had said, about his Ijaw origin. But no one knew his real name. So, Asampete conferred with some Ijaw residents, including Ray, and chose a name for him: Worimegbei. Her name became Asampete Worimegbei.

She organized a special memorial service for her father and had picture posters of him pasted all over Kaita Beach. The Development Board had the posters removed and asked her to leave. Shanka intervened. Asampete then founded the Quiet Academy for Children. Segi gave her a room on the upper floor of the Bonus Club, and they became great friends. Ray became her "brother." Idi and Orita became her "uncles" and they told her innumerable stories that her father had presumably told them.

Quiet, according to Idi, was once given two coins by his

mother on a Sunday morning – one for himself, the other for the church offering. As he trotted off to church, rolling his wheel along, his pastime as a boy, one of the coins fell into the bush. He searched for it in vain. "Well, God in heaven," he said to the sky. "You wey dey see everything, that coin na for you; this na my own."

Orita had a story about how Quiet as a boy had been fond of pinching a few coins from the offertory basket while pretending to be putting in his own offering. One day, as he was about to do so, the choir began a new song:

> He has come again
>
> Holy Spirit, he has come again

Alarmed, Quite bolted from the church. That was why, he said, Quiet always kept awake during the offertory procession in his years as a churchwarden.

"I knew I was right when I decided to set up a café in New Maroko," Prinzi told Ashikodi. "Look at what's happening. It's the Nigerian story writing itself before my eyes. What more can a writer ask for?"

"The stamina to do the actual writing."

"Look who's talking of stamina, you runaway..."

"My friend, my fate has seized me."

"At the Bonus Club?"

"The beginning of the world. And Segi was the first woman that God made. That's why He kept her for so long in the Great Garden before He reluctantly sent her, His masterpiece, to the world."

"Is that why she's still housing that temptation, Asampete, whom I hear has become Shanka's lover?"

"World people! What will the slum be without its tattles? Anyway, you know Segi. She's like the Freedom Square."

"The latitude to be, eh? But this sounds to me like sleeping with the enemy."

"Not necessarily the same as marching with the enemy."

"Go on, argue the difference. But that Shanka, he certainly has an eye for beauty."

"That's probably why he abandoned hunting. There's no beauty in the forest, except for those who can see with the eyes of the spirit."

"The 'Roko!"

"You know, I prefer compliments from the brewery, bottled."

"Be sure to remind me tomorrow."

"And tomorrow and the day after. You'll never change, you protector of the breweries."

"That's your pocket talking. Anyway, I hear Shanka wants to change all the signposts in town to read 'Kaita Beach.'"

"Whether they call it Kaita Beach or Kaabiyesi's Kingdom or even Haile's Shrine, this place will always be Maroko. Just like New Queenstown."

"Well, I've decided to put up a signpost."

"You?"

"A big signpost that will say 'Prinzi's Café, NEW MAROKO.'"

And he did, at the same time that Shanka had 'Kaita Beach' written on all the signposts in the settlement, with a crocodile imprint beside the name. At about the same time, Razaki announced a New Maroko Weekend Special at the Bonus Club – a "musical theater" featuring Segi and Ashikodi, with himself as the artistic director. In response, the Good Evening Hotel, which underwent another metamorphosis and became The Pant Academy, announced Special Makossa Nights promising "heavy Congo music" and a striptease.

Kaita Beach looked set for a swinging time.

The New Maroko Weekend Special mainly consisted of Segi and Ashikodi doing named dances. The Madam Bonus Dance had them orbiting the stage in a waist and groin performance charged with sensualism; Ignatius was a river dance in which Ashikodi played the canoeist and Segi the mermaid; Goomsi a wind dance in which they became like a sandstorm. Razaki bustled about seeing to the lighting and stage effects – the bursts of smoke, the sound of the river, the roar of the wind, the costumes, the music – and generally ensuring that everything went well.

The auditorium brimmed over.

Asampete asked to be allowed to do the Quiet Dance, which included her gliding about the stage like a tempting prayer. Razaki then added the Charity Dance, during which Segi and Ashikodi swayed on each other's body, sometimes with one person almost leaning backward to touch the ground. The Omo-ale dance, which was the next addition, featured Ray monkeying around the stage.

The fame of the Bonus Club and the New Maroko Weekend Special spread. As the crowd, including many non-residents, became almost a flood, Razaki decided on two shows – an early night revue and a midnight performance. While the club continued to admit residents gratis, it began to charge an entrance fee from non-residents.

Shanka became an occasional guest. Razaki mooted the idea of refusing him admission. Segi rejected it, opting instead to have him pay the same admission fee as non-residents.

Prinzi and One were regular guests.

"You know," he said to her one night, "everyone is now creatively engaged, except me. What am I even waiting for – the marriage of Kaabiyesi?"

He stayed up all night wrestling with the first page of his New Maroko novel. By dawn, he had destroyed almost a whole ream of paper but produced only one sentence acceptable to him: *The Bonus Club was the heartbeat of Maroko.*

"Don't worry," empathized One. "Little by little."

"If only I could write the first paragraph..."

One wrapped herself around him, and a dream of another kind rose like fire in Prinzi's being.

Fourteen

The dust storm seized Kaita Beach by the throat one morning. Swirling clouds of dust danced the conga, as Ashikodi would say, round the settlement, threatening to uproot it and smash it out of ordered existence. No one, apart from Ashikodi perhaps, had ever witnessed such a frightening spectacle. The residents promptly took refuge behind locked doors.

"It's as if the world is about to come to an end, *abi* how you see am, Miracle?" Linda asked Ray.

"Just leave me alone this morning."

"I see-e, getting ready for Judgement Day and feeling afraid?" she said with a laugh she did not feel. "Me too. All of us. But since Asampete come, e be like say your head don dey correct. Maybe you go get reduced sentence."

"Look, leave me a-l-o-n-e. I go shout-o!"

The dust storm coated Kaita Beach with more filth than it was used to. It smashed windows and doors, tore roofs apart as if they were paper ribbons, and destroyed the abattoir. The people counted themselves lucky that no one was borne away by the storm or blinded or torn apart. Still, they were surprised when DJ Oris the Dazzle announced that the dust storm had clipped the tail of one of the stone crocodiles on Kaabiyesi Island. Kaabiyesi, according to the announcement, had decided to fast for three hundred and thirty days and to sacrifice one of his ninety-eight-year-old fingernails. And it was his wish that the fingernail be buried in Shanka Square.

"People of the kingdom, sanctify yourselves, therefore, for the burial of Kaabiyesi's priceless fingernail tomorrow at dusk. No plastic wreaths, please."

The funeral began with the arrival of a procession bearing a small, ornamented coffin from the direction of Kaabiyesi Island. There were six clean-shaven men, whom no one had ever seen before. Each of them was dressed in a white wrapper, red beads, and white and red feathers. All were barefooted. The two that walked side by side at the front of the procession and the two at the rear carried orbs of incense. The two in the middle bore the coffin. As they approached, they chanted a dirge in an unknown language. Making their way with measured steps toward Shanka Square, they resembled antediluvian priests or shrine keepers.

They set the coffin down beside a tomb, which had been erected by the entrance to the square, and began to go round the tomb. They did so seven times. Then Shanka and Kaita made funeral orations extolling Kaabiyesi's public spirit in sacrificing his fingernail to stop the dust storm and to mourn the damage to the sacred stone crocodile.

The six coffin bearers rendered a drawn-out dirge. Thereafter, the burial took place. And the coffin bearers departed the way they had come, the two that had borne the coffin now carrying palm fronds.

The tombstone bore the legend: Kaabiyesi's Fingernail, 1900-1998.

"That, certainly, is one burial that should enter the Book of Records," mused Prinzi. "All that for a fingernail, which no one even saw! Kaabiyesi sacrificed his fingernail to stop the dust storm? Indeed!"

"Well, they've had theirs," said Ashikodi. "We should have ours. We should bury something – a stick, a cigarette stub or something like that."

"Why not bury something that has blood?" suggested Asampete, who had arrived with Segi.

"That's a very good idea, Asa," said Segi. "Come to think of it, why not Mar?"

"Mm-mm," protested Centigrade. "Please, leave Mar out of this."

"Mar! That's a brilliant idea," Prinzi said.

"I don't think it should be an ordinary burial," added Ashikodi. "We should have a second burial, which is usually reserved for chiefs."

"And how do you think the Development Board will

respond?" asked Asampete.

"Shanka is the de facto head of the Development Board, and he would most probably monitor the event but not disrupt it."

"You're now an expert on Shanka?" Prinzi asked Ashikodi.

"Does anyone realize what these people are really doing?" asked Ashikodi, ignoring Prinzi's question. "The announcement that Kaabiyesi has decided to fast for three hundred and thirty days was the key that I had been on the lookout for."

"And what door did it open?"

"You know that Kaita and Shanka are Kanuris. One of Kaita's ancestors was a commander in the Kanem-Bornu Empire under ldris Alooma, who reputedly staged a total of three hundred and thirty campaigns. These people are re-enacting here – for their own profit – the stations of the cross, so to speak, of the Kanem-Bornu Empire."

"The 'Roko! And they're doing that with Kaabiyesi, a Yoruba figure?"

"That's a smokescreen, or an adaptation. Kaabiyesi represents the sacred monarch, who was worshipped but almost never seen. His crocodiles represent the sacred snake of the Kanuri ancestral religion. Think of the achievements of Dunama II, Ali Ghaji, Idris Alooma. Each expanded the radius of the kingdom. Isn't that what is going on here – the conquest of New Maroko?"

"But why the Kanem-Bornu Empire?"

"Because it's what they know. They don't represent an ethnic mafia. No. These people are profiteers; they will exploit anything in order to make a killing."

"So, was it an all-male thing?" asked Asampete.

"Idris Alooma survived because of the political savvy and determination of a woman, Magira Aisa, who protected him from danger and secured the regency of Bornu until he came of age."

"That's good to hear."

"You see the power of history?" Ashikodi said deliberately to Prinzi.

And so the burial of Kaabiyesi's fingernail was followed by

the "second burial" of "His Excellency, Prince Mar of Maroko."

The symbolic burial, which involved a grave and a coffin but no corpse, took place outside Centigrade's door. A condolence book was opened beneath a framed picture of Mar. Razaki played the role of a pastor. Segi and Ashikodi sang an elegy. Centigrade delivered the graveside oration. Chief Tanker and Orita were the gravediggers. Prinzi served some free drinks. Asampete saw to the food. Opio staged a special performance. And the burial became a carnival.

The Development Board pretended the event never happened. Shanka surprised everyone by calling on Centigrade the next day to offer his condolences. He stopped by Prinzi's Café afterwards.

"Hmm, a visit from Olympus," Prinzi said with sarcasm. "How are the gods these days?"

Shanka smiled. "I'm not a messenger of the gods," he said. "You and I know that."

"Does my name sound like Kaita?"

"Do not take his name in vain."

"Really? Look, what do you want here? This is a bar, of course, but we hear you have a bigger one in your beach resort."

"Oh, I'm sure you would know about that. Well, I've come to pay my respects and to wish you well."

"I'm well, thank you."

"I bring you good tidings from Kaita Alhaji Kaita the Magnificent. He's interested in your welfare. And here's a special medallion from Kaabiyesi the Great. He regrets he could not see you on the day you visited, but this is a sign that he has you in his thoughts."

Prinzi declined the offer. "No, and no, and no. Do you take me for Haile or what?"

"You're speaking the language of the trench. Why? We're community developers, nothing more."

"Well, I have something for your Kaabiyesi." He proffered a cork. "It will restore his fingernail. Good day."

Shanka took the cork, examined it closely, then dropped it on the floor and departed.

The day after the encounter, anonymous posters headlined "The True Story of Kaita" appeared on the walls of Shanka Square. Each poster had a picture of Kaita in a prison uniform.

"Pictures don't lie," read the posters. "This man is a criminal. He is wanted by the police in four countries for forgery, rape, attempted murder, and Obtaining by Trick (OBT). That is why he is hiding in New Maroko. His mother was a market thief. His father was a breeder of vultures. He was reared on vulture meat. Perhaps that is why he loves carcasses. Beware!"

Kaita described the posters as "absolute bunkum" in a special interview on Radio Kaabiyesi. The Development Board quickly had the posters removed and wrote a "final warning letter" to Prinzi for "participation and suspected participation in activities likely to cause a breach of the peace in Kaita Beach."

And then, as if from the dead, Alhaja Osunwunmi reappeared. She had grown tired of living abroad and had returned to Faith Villa in New Queenstown. After some time, she had decided to visit her former tenants. She had another motive though. The first place she was driven to in the long, wide-bodied vehicle that brought her was Kaita's mansion. There, she held a "closed door" meeting with Kaita and Shanka.

As usual, she was quite a spectacle, what with her headgear that seemed to be a maze of circles, her loopy earrings, innumerable bracelets, and a dress that looked like an Afro-Brazilian ritual costume.

"I've been to the palace," she said when she arrived at Prinzi's Café, "and I decided to look in on the opposition. How are you these days, Mr Prinzi?"

"I'm keeping well," a surprised Prinzi responded. "And you?"

"I'm fine, I hope. I could be better, I know."

"Actually, you shine like the sun."

"Thank you. Flattery hurts no one. That's one of the good

things about being home. I've been in Europe since. All the time I was there, it was 'How do you do?' and 'How do you do?' all over again. I was homesick from the day I arrived."

Prinzi said nothing.

"I came to see Alhaji Kaita and the other fellow, Shanka. I was referred to them by some of my friends in government, but it seems even they cannot help me get the compensation I was promised, not to talk of recovering my land."

"You mean you've not been compensated?"

"Oh no, I've not. Alhaji Kaita is my neighbor in New Queenstown, or whatever it is they call Maroko now. He has a truly palatial residence there, and I know his family fairly well, although he himself prefers to spend a lot of time here."

"So, how come Kaabiyesi Investments has been compensated for New Maroko?"

"Political connections, I suppose."

"You know they've changed the name of the settlement from New Maroko to Kaita Beach?"

"They don't understand. Maroko goes a long way back. It started with The Mark, our foremost ancestor. Although his name was Awolowo, he became known as The Mark because it had been prophesied before his birth that he would be a sage and that his coming would mark his community's ascension. He later became an interpreter at the court of the King of Brazil and helped many families settle there, especially in Bahia. He was known as Marak in Brazil, and to this day there is still Marak Quarters in Bahia, around the area where he lived and is buried. Eventually, one of his grandsons decided to return home. He settled in the area until recently known as Maroko. People found 'Marak' rather strange, so they began calling the place Maraki. By the time the name got down to me, it had become Maroko. Now, it's all gone. They're calling it something like New Queenstown; here, it's Kaita Beach."

"A great pity, madam, but it seems someone is rooting his own family tree."

"Well, this I've learned from aging: nothing endures

forever. You watch and see: those who conspired to shoot down the son of the sun shall swim in pieces."

Prinzi reached for his pen and notebook.

"I, Alhaja Lateefat Awolowo-Maraki-Osunwunmi, I have put a curse on them in the shrine of my ancestors, and I see them floating in the flood. You watch and see."

Prinzi crossed himself after her departure and called in both One and Centigrade to tell them about the experience.

Alhaja Osunwunmi took to visiting Kaita Beach and soon adopted Asampete as her "daughter."

The next returnee was Pastor David. Instead of the dapper appearance for which he had been known, he wore a threadbare suit and carried a thumb-worn Bible. Gradually, his story spread. He was said to have moved to Brazilian Quarters after the demolition of Maroko and soon had a song and dance going on there. His fame had spread and he had prospered. But his congregation demanded miracles – and more miracles. In his desperation to satisfy this swelling hunger, he made a pact that led to his burial of a live goat in his church. He prospered all the more, making him the envy of other preachers in the area. All sorts of uncomplimentary stories about him soon began to circulate. When the burial was finally exposed, his congregation transformed into an irreverent mob. And he had to vamoose in order to escape being set ablaze, the mob payback for swindlers and criminals popular in that part of Lagos. He then made his way to New Maroko.

He still had his histrionics and could still send tingles down the spine with his preaching.

"Look at me, people, l-o-o-k at me!" he declaimed. "I am the Job of the New World, the miracle of transformation the Lord has sent to minister to the soul of this generation. They persecute me because I serve the Lord. But I will not forsake the temple of my Father. Even though I walk now in the valley, I tell you: His banner over me, still, is love, and He will bless me richly according to my suffering. I serve the Light of the World. I serve the Paragon of Justice. I serve the living God. Brethren and sisters, we serve the

God of riches. Come on, people, c-o-m-e o-n, sing it:

> "Praising the Lord
> Always
> Praising the Lord
> With all my heart
> Praising the Lord
> With all my heart
> Always
> Hallelujah
> My Lord is good
> Hallelujah
> My Lord is good
> My Lord is good
> He's good to me."

As he sang, tears flowed from his eyes and he tore his hair as if he alone was atoning for the sins of the world. The people marveled at how effortlessly he had given back to the settlement something that it had lost – the incantatory passion and hypnotic drama of religion. With the return of the Church of David, all the other churches – and there were many, as many as there were brothels and bars – entered a period of decline.

Asampete offered Pastor David the use of the Quiet Academy for Children on weekends. He named her Fortunata.

"You are blessed among women," he told her. "You will see how richly the Lord will bless you."

Even Chief Tanker, Kaita Beach's most notorious drinker, desired to become part of his congregation.

"The Lord will bless you too," Pastor David told him. "But first you must put away your talisman."

"Talisman?"

"Your tortoise necklace. It's not of God."

"I know. Na from Jesse I carry am come."

"You must put it away. So says the Lord."

"No vex-o, pastor, maybe you no hear the thing wey the Lord talk well well. This tortoise na God Imself say make I carry am from Jesse so that people go know my story, know say anywhere wey God destroy the world E go leave some people behind make them dey remember."

Pastor David regarded him for some time. "You're not ready for the kingdom yet," he told him. "Better make haste. The end time is drawing nigh."

"E don pass already for Jesse."

Opio, whom Pastor David had described as "the priest of a dead shrine," congratulated Chief Tanker for his "better Urhobo sense." He took to blowing a powdery substance in the direction of the church.

"You see this powder so?" he would announce to passersby. "Na me and that una Pastor David. Na run e go run comot for here. You go see. This na Biafra magic wey even Zik of Africa himself follow formulate. When we blow am p-h-u-a-m like this, the enemy must fall. How you think say we kill plenty Nigerian soldiers for Uzuakoli?"

Despite Opio's antics, and to the amazement of people like Prinzi, the Church of David bloomed. Ray became a warden, Iya Idi a devout member. Centigrade suddenly remembered that his original name was Chukwukadibia: God is greater than the medicine man. Idi "showed face" from time to time. Even Shanka put in an appearance once in a while. Gradually, Pastor David became his old dapper self.

"I am the miracle of the Lord's vineyard," he proclaimed. "And many more shall hear, come, and marvel. I am the return that beckons."

It was like a conjuration. Mama Badejo returned with her children. She had become darker in complexion and her brow more furrowed. She danced about the settlement, marveling at how the people had survived. She rented two rooms in Centigrade's new house and reestablished her beancake business. Opio became one of her regular customers. It was not long before the rumor began making the rounds about a romance between the two.

"Maroko people, una no go ever change? I been think say

here na Kaita Beach" was Mama Badejo's response.

"Idle civilians at work," Opio said disdainfully.

Iya Idi was gladdened by her friend's return. And she led her back to the Church of David.

"Are you sure this man has not buried a live elephant in his church this time around?" Prinzi said to One.

"The poor must have their God. I'm quoting you."

Prompted by Asampete, Alhaja Osunwunmi stopped by Mama Badejo's beancake kiosk. And that was how one of Mama Badejo's daughters went to work in Faith Villa as a housemaid so she could go to school in New Queenstown. Pastor David claimed the "victory": "Remember the check I gave you at Maroko? It's about to mature. You must pray and fast – and praise the Lord." Opio denounced him and added pepper to the powdery mixture he blew at the church. Mama Badejo became a devoted member of the congregation.

She had returned, she said, because the village had not been kind to her.

"To be widow for Nigeria na *wahala*. To be double widow...ah, the things wey my eyes see..."

She had begun to plan her return when she met someone who had been to New Maroko and who confirmed that the people had not disappeared from the face of the earth, as she had feared.

"I thank God say I no loss my children for village-o. Na so small small children dey born like say to get belly na to lick ice cream. For night, na so them dey pio pio pio for corner. The boys, some don get pass PhD to steal yam and fowl. You know how many people wey confess say they be witch the time when I dey there? Today, this; tomorrow, that. How this country come spoil like this?"

She was just in time for the next sensation in Kaita Beach – the discovery of oil, or so the story went. A survey team appeared in the settlement one morning, and that was all that was needed to encourage speculations that there was oil in Kaita Beach. Chief Tanker, who had arrogated to himself the status of the local authority on such matters, helped talk up the possibility.

"I for talk am since," he declared. "The water here just be like the water for Jesse, like say oil dey leak for under ground dey join the water. Even sef, na as this tortoise, Nyerhovwo, dey behave when e near water here na so im mama been dey do for Jesse."

The rumor brought several reporters to Kaita Beach. Efe was one of them.

"I hear you fellows are about to become oil barons," she said with a burst of laughter at Prinzi's Café. "A team of survey students on a project appears and Kaita Beach – that's the correct name, right? – thinks it's about to become Saudi Arabia."

"Forget that the people mistook a survey class for oil explorers," said Prinzi. "There could be oil here, you know. I've been doing some reading lately, technical stuff."

"Oh yes, the professor of molecular geology speaks of oil wells," remarked Ashikodi.

"Gentlemen," Efe cut in before Prinzi could respond, "if an oil discovery is made here now, it would be good timing. There's a powerful lobby to have resource rights returned to individual landowners, with the government only collecting taxes. If that succeeds, all the natural resources here will automatically be the property of Kaabiyesi Investments. And you know what else? I've made an interesting discovery. There's a link between Omo-ale and Kaita. Both were classmates."

"You're a marvel."

The reporter beamed. "There must be some kind of oil here. Oil is the instrument of power in this country."

Fifteen

The dissolution of the Development Board was accomplished through a radio announcement. The radio statement simply stated: "His Excellency, the Military Governor of Lagos State, Colonel Raji Omo-ale, has ordered the dissolution of the New Maroko Development Board with immediate effect. A sole administrator for Kaita Beach Local Government Area will be named in due course."

Kaita Beach Local Government Area?

Later in the day, another statement clarified that, yes, "the Federal Government of Nigeria has approved the creation of Kaita Beach Local Government Area made up of Kaita Beach, Kaabiyesi Island, Coconut Island, and Tarzan Jetty – with headquarters in Kaita Beach." Chief Haile Manafiki was named the sole administrator.

Many Kaita Beach residents turned up the next day at the office of the Development Board to boo the handover to a robust Haile, who looked like a bank manager in a double-breasted suit. Apart from the singing of the national anthem, the event consisted of the lowering of the signpost of the Development Board and the hoisting of a new signpost painted in the national colors. The new signpost proclaimed: Kaita Beach Local Government Area Headquarters. Sole Administrator: Chief Haile Manafiki, BA (Hons).

Haile had arrived that morning from the direction of Kaabiyesi Island in an air-conditioned car with tinted glasses accompanied by drummers, dancers, and policemen. He had met with Kaita and Shanka at the Palace of Good and inspected his new living quarters – Shanka's former residence – before being driven to his new office.

After the handover ceremony, members of the Development Board took their leave, Haile retreated inside, and the police dispersed the crowd. DJ Oris the Dazzle announced that

Haile would make a broadcast that evening and would tour the settlement the next day "to feel the pulse of the people."

Kaita Beach waited with wonder and anxiety.

"Greetings to you, fellow citizens of Kaita Beach Local Government Area. I, Chief Haile Manafiki, on behalf of the new Kaita Beach Local Government, hereby address you. In response to our yearning for rapid development, the government has created Kaita Beach Local Government Area and appointed me its sole administrator. I am, as you all know, an apostle of rapid development.

"We will commence with immediate effect the execution of our rolling plan for social and economic development. The incinerator is hereby shut with immediate effect. All the workers affected will be absorbed by the Kaita Beach Waste Management Authority, which will explore more environment-friendly methods of waste disposal.

"Under this new dispensation, all residents have an important role to play. A development tax, in addition to other taxes, is hereby imposed on all adults. Meanwhile, we have initiated the construction of a police station with an appropriate detention facility in order to boost security.

"Thank you and remain blessed."

The next day when Haile stopped by Prinzi's Café during his "familiarization tour" of Kaita Beach, he met Prinzi, Ashikodi, Razaki, and Centigrade. Ashikodi sang a nursery rhyme when he entered:

> John Bull, my son
> I sent you to school
> You don't know how to spell 'John Bull'
> 'J-o-h-n B-u-l-l'
> That's the way to spell 'John Bull'

"The one that never changes," Haile said with a chuckle, then he asked his entourage to wait outside. "What's that all about? Am I interrupting a kindergarten?"

Ashikodi's response was another song:

O meo, O meo
O meo meo meo
I've come to tell you
About a certain war
The people of Ashanti
They have no sense
When they and the royals
Came to blows
They shouted:
Meo meo!

"What are you trying to tell me, Mr 'Roko?" Haile asked.

"'John Bull' is too simple for you, 'Meo Meo' too complex. What then do you know? You're John Bull back from school in Kaabiyesi Island..."

"A fattening house too," Prinzi noted.

"And you're like those colonials who would go to Bini and teach them to sing that the people of Ashanti have no sense, then go to Ashanti and teach them the same thing about the Binis. You're both the pupil and the lie."

"To the people of Prinzi's Café: greetings" was Haile's unexpected reply.

"I listened to your broadcast, Haile," said Razaki. "Taxes and levies, levies and taxes. Is that what you call 'government'?"

"Em, em...Chief Haile here..." began Centigrade, who looked otherworldly in a French suit.

"Better behave yourself before I throw you out," Prinzi snarled at him. "Is this all you can be, Haile – another pawn?"

"And what are you?" Haile snapped. "You sit here and shoot down everything. Unlike you, I'm not afraid to dare, even to dare to be wrong."

"Hurrah, the dare!" sneered Ashikodi.

Centigrade looked from one to the other, then he calmly led the sole administrator out of the café. At the door, Haile turned round and, with a clenched fist, uttered a slogan that baffled everyone: "Power to the people!"

The next day, Prinzi, Razaki, and Ashikodi collected signatures from Segi, Asampete, Ray, Chief Tanker, Opio, Mama Badejo, One, a reluctant Centigrade, and many other residents, then they filed a lawsuit against Haile and his government to forestall its new tax regime. The case was thrown out for "lack of jurisdiction."

Meanwhile, Tony St Oris, formerly DJ Oris the Dazzle, became Haile's Special Assistant. A new presenter took over at Kaabiyesi Radio, a young woman who was fond of false eyelashes. She gave her name as Cassandra the Cute, "or Double C for short."

Pastor David conceived the idea of an improvement union. That Sunday, he preached a long sermon exhorting Kaita Beach to take its destiny in its own hands. "That is the way forward. To live forever in the past is to die forever to the present and to abort the future." His congregation nodded, under his influence. The pastor glowed, already structuring in his mind how he would combine his evangelical duties with the chairmanship of the Kaita Beach Improvement Union.

When he convened the first meeting of the union at Shanka Square, however, he was taken aback by the ferocity of the opposition.

"Kaita Beach is a fat lie," declared Prinzi. "Shanka Square, Kaita Beach, Haile's Gate – yes, I hear there's a plan to rename the entrance gate. Why are all these happening? They're attempts to reinvent our experience, to reinvent us. Names are important because they're charged with meaning. An improvement union, yes, but why not a New Maroko Improvement Union?"

"Brother Prinzi," Pastor David appealed. "We must be wary of an exercise in futility. A New Maroko Improvement Union is unlikely to receive official approval. And why do we dwell on the past as if our experience has foreclosed the present and the future?"

"Do we need 'official approval'?" asked Razaki. "The denial of being is only possible where there is no conviction or unity."

"And why should we not make much of the past?" queried

Ashikodi. "Of course, one can understand why a fraud like you would want to deny or understate the past, but really..."

"You call me a fraud, you? You ne'er-do-well, you dare stand up in the assembly of the brethren and blaspheme against a servant of the living God?"

Segi and Asampete managed to stop the heated exchange from degenerating into fisticuffs.

"Why do we quarrel among ourselves?" Segi said. "Our princes and emperors cut our throats without raising their voices, yet we argue with thunder about even our own name. Pastor, you have to understand why Kaita Beach is a difficult name for us to accept. When they mowed us down in Maroko, we went through hell without the anesthesia of death. We're the children of twilight. How can we forget the dusk?"

Prinzi's fury paled as he scribbled away, looking fondly at Segi. Razaki suppressed a smile.

"A beach," ventured Centigrade, speaking like a dictionary, "is the seashore, often developed into a tour...ist ground, like the famous Copa Cabana Beach in Brazil. It sounds e...xo...tic, but, well, if the autho...rities..."

"For a man professedly in the sciences," Prinzi cut him short, "you're miserly with straight talk. We're not discussing the authorities here. We're discussing a people taking their destiny in their own hands."

"E get as e be," said Chief Tanker. "If person wake up tomorrow say they wan begin call Jesse Kesse, we people no go 'gree-o, because Jesse na the name wey our ancestors give our place and na their blood na im dey our body."

"Exactly," agreed Pastor David. "In this case, it's the same people who own this land that have changed the name. After all, whose ancestor here chose the name 'Maroko'?"

Heads swiveled in all directions in search of an absent Alhaja Osunwunmi.

"You see-e," continued Pastor David. "And Jesse's own case is different, because Jesse is in the Bible, the Word of God."

"Jesse dey for Bible?" Chief Tanker beamed, then his face fell. "So, why God come allow one t-h-o-u-s-a-n-d people plus just perish like that? *Abi* e dey break that time?"

"Temptation shall come, but woe to he through whom temptation comes," Pastor David quoted at him. "Beware of temptation, brother. Beware of blasphemy, because the God who maketh you to stand and speak can just as easily strike you lame and dumb."

"In which case He should be arrested," Ashikodi said deliberately.

Words failed Pastor David. He stared, openmouthed, at the offender.

Asampete suggested a compromise: New Maroko/Kaita Beach Improvement Union. Neither Pastor David nor Prinzi and his fellows were quite satisfied, but they accepted the suggestion – "as a starting point," noted Prinzi.

Pastor David then called for a vote to decide who would head the union, counseling that godliness should guide the choice of a leader "so that God will bless us according to our choice." He wanted an open ballot. Prinzi opposed the idea. Asampete, who was unanimously chosen as the returning officer, opted for a secret ballot.

The votes overwhelmingly favored Ashikodi. Questioning the fairness of the electoral process, Pastor David immediately objected. The next day, he sent a protest letter to the Sole Administrator. Two days later, an unsigned statement from the office of the Special Assistant declared the result inconclusive and annulled the election. Ashikodi derided the announcement, but when he attempted to convene his first meeting as the chairman of the union, he was arrested.

He spent one week in detention in New Queenstown before his release. Upon his return, he attempted to convene another meeting. Only Segi, Prinzi, and Razaki attended. Nevertheless, he became known as Chairman 'Roko or 'Roko the Chair.

The attention of Kaita Beach had been seized by events at The Pant Academy. The Syrian founder, Kamal, and his estranged Nigerian wife were locked in an ownership battle. Kamal had been wrongly deported just before the exodus from Maroko. Adlyn, his wife, had taken over the management and overseen the relocation of the hotel's moveable assets. Upon his return, Kamal attempted to take over the brothel. Adlyn was determined not to let him, so Kamal brought in the police. Adlyn accomplished the incredible: she obtained a court injunction, within the hour, against Kamal and the police.

However, the police had already turned the brothel upside down – and discovered World Bank holed up in Caro's room. He was wanted in connection with a prisonbreak, but he was determined not to be returned to prison. In the ensuing gunfight, he killed two policemen before he was translated into an obituary report in the newspapers. Despite the court injunction, The Pant Academy was sealed up.

A report in one of the independent newspapers described World Bank as "a known associate of Shanka El Shanka." The former leader of the hunters' guild in Maroko denied any such relationship and sued the paper for character assassination. He was eventually pacified with a front-page apology. Centigrade thanked his God effusively and even held a solemn "celebration of life" at Prinzi's Café. "Even though I walk through the valley of the shadow of death," he recited, "I shall fear no evil, for the Lord is my shepherd."

Haile rose to the occasion by speeding up the construction of a police station with an "appropriate detention facility." The first detainee was Efe. She was arrested on her way to Prinzi's Café. No reason was given.

Prinzi, Ashikodi, and Razaki rallied the residents for a march on the police station to demand her immediate release. The march became a sit-in, with the protesters sitting outside the police station and singing heady songs. The sit-in lasted three days before the detainee regained her freedom. Her dismissal from the government paper was announced over the radio. No reason was given.

At this time, Radio Kaabiyesi announced the "discovery" of oil "in commercial quantities" in and around Kaabiyesi Island.

"A very good morning to you, people of the kingdom," twittered Double C. "With maximum pleasure, the Sole Administrator has announced the discovery of oil in commercial quantities in and around Kaabiyesi Island. This is the big time, people. So, rise and shine. Remain blessed."

"You see what I've been saying all along?" Efe said at Prinzi's Café.

"So, oil. Oil exploration is the preserve of the federal government. How does that help our local fat cats?"

"If the government lets go of oil rights, then they'll have everything – both the land and the oil. Even if the government doesn't let go, this is going to be one of the richest local government areas in the country – not for the people though."

"It's all becoming clearer. So, why Kaabiyesi?"

"Because they had to anchor their right to the land and divert everyone's attention, I think. There's nothing like an ancestral figure, or age and tradition, to establish land ownership. Land and ancestors go together, haven't you noticed? Which is why people fight heedless battles for little turfs where their ancestor stopped to drink at a well or paused to shake his fist at the sky."

"You know, Efe, you're deep."

"That's nice to hear from the great Prinzi himself."

"My friend, Razaki..."

"Oh yeah? You're also a matchmaker?"

"Not that, but I can interpret what I see and hear. Anyway, if there's oil in and around Kaabiyesi Island, then Kaabiyesi himself has to move. That should be very interesting and an opportunity to unmask him once and for all."

Sixteen

Despite the preceding rumors and even the knowledge that Ashikodi had lately begun to spend the night in Segi's bedroom, the announcement of the marriage still took many residents of Kaita Beach unawares. The marriage of Segilola – to Ashikodi!

"Listen, people," Ashikodi himself announced at the marketplace. "For centuries, the earth has been orbiting around the sun. But for one day this week, it will stand still for the sun and the moon will be conjoined forever. Her name is Segi, the eye of sunlight. My name is Ashikodi, the son of the wind, the moon, and the stars. We'll become one, and this will be the marker that the world has been waiting for. Do you hear me, people?"

Shanka offered to sponsor the wedding. Ashikodi declined the offer. Nevertheless, Shanka sent two cows, a male and a female, as a wedding present. Kaita sent a truckload of foodstuff. The couple had the foodstuff and the cows shared among residents of Coconut Island and Kaita Beach. Alhaja Osunwunmi accepted to give away the bride, Razaki to play the role of an impresario. Asampete was to be the bridesmaid. Prinzi, whom Ashikodi chose as his best man, announced that the first edition of his novel on Maroko would be issued on that day. Opio promised a performance of the Biafran resurrection, Mama Badejo, a basket of beancakes.

The next day, Prinzi put up a handwritten notice at the entrance to his café announcing the title of his novel: *Invisible Chapters*.

"Such a long journey for only two words," said Ashikodi, referring to the many titles that Prinzi had celebrated and discarded on the road to his final decision. The cover illustration depicted a man standing on his palms, with the sun peeping out from between his legs. Razaki, who had hoped to produce a drama sketch for the occasion, sat at his desk for three nights but only succeeded in holding an unprofitable argument with a pile of blank paper. He gave up with the declaration that "the drama of a wedding should suffice."

The day finally arrived.

Radio Kaabiyesi surprisingly heralded the event with a special broadcast, which Double C began by playing a Swahili song, *Malaika Nakupenda*: 'I love you, angel.' She then went on and on, quoting from a book purportedly written by Kaabiyesi about marriage and responsibility. Neither Ashikodi's nor Segi's name was mentioned. Ashikodi renamed the station "Radio Bunkum."

The ceremony at the marriage registry was brief. Almost every adult in Kaita Beach was there to bear witness. Haile stopped by to congratulate the couple.

"I and I is love, still?" Ashikodi asked him.

"Always. Love, always."

"All God's children got wings, eh?" mused Prinzi.

After the signing of the marriage certificate, the party then moved to the Bonus Club, which had been festooned. Once there, the celebration took on a life of its own. With quite an extravaganza going on – Opio's performance, Alhaja Osunwunmi's Afro-Brazilian dance, a display by the drummers and acrobats that had accompanied Ashikodi from Coconut Island, Chief Tanker's "Jesse memorial" – nourished by a surfeit of food and wine, Razaki had to make several appeals in order to create the atmosphere for the nuptial dance. It was the New Maroko Weekend Special reinvented as the Passion of Segi and Ashikodi.

Finally, Prinzi was given the opportunity to present his book. There was only one copy, "a special wedding present to a special couple on a special occasion in the life of New Maroko – the seemingly invisible chapters of dreams at work."

Ashikodi publicly thanked him for the gift but called him aside to "discuss" the "fraud." "*Invisible Chapters* on the cover and two hundred blank pages as the invisible text. Is this all, Prinzi?"

"Not on your life. Just the pre-text edition."

"The writer takes refuge in a pre-text and condemns the

story of our lives to chapters of dumb pages?" Ashikodi said drily. "Surely, you're a candidate for a Failed Books Tribunal. Your book of everything is finally unveiled as an unreadable book of nothing."

He rejoined Segi whistling "Segi the 'Kodi" and the couple retired. The celebration continued, further enlivened by the arrival of a band sent by Shanka, until far into the night. That night, Radio Kaabiyesi played *Malaika Nakupenda* and ran another commentary on the wedding that mentioned and congratulated the couple.

The days that followed passed by in relative peace, and the residents began to plan for Christmas, their second outside Maroko. There were talks about another procession to New Queenstown, but they died down when the police issued a warning that any such movement "into or out of" Kaita Beach without a permit would be forcefully disbanded. Shanka set the opening of the Kaita Beach Resort for Christmas Eve. A Father Christmas Committee – constituted mainly by members of the waterfront fraternity – sprang up, concerned with how to make the season profitable to its members. Pastor David announced a Christmas Day Holy Spirit Carnival: "All who come shall receive, all!" Radio Kaabiyesi began playing a song, "Christmas Polka," that only a few of the residents had ever heard before. And the harmattan season set in, with its dry wind and red dust.

It was at this time, two weeks to Christmas Eve, that a storm surge devastated Kaabiyesi Island. While the surge and the whereabouts of Kaabiyesi became the dominant public inquiry, Haile, Shanka, and Kaita shuttled between Kaita Beach and Kaabiyesi Island in a flying boat. Meanwhile, the tales grew heads and tails. Some said that Kaabiyesi's kin, who had grown weary of awaiting his return, had escorted him home to the ocean depths. Some others claimed that Kaabiyesi had relocated to Tarzan Jetty just before the surge. Among the Prinzi Café fraternity, the opinion was that perhaps Kaabiyesi was nowhere to be seen or heard from because he had never been.

Radio Kaabiyesi, which had begun a continuous broadcast

of martial music at dawn, finally broke the news at midday.

"Children of the kingdom, it is with a very heavy heart that I, Kaita Alhaji Kaita, announce the passing away to greater glory of our father and benefactor, Kaabiyesi the Great. Consequent on the storm surge, which destroyed Kaabiyesi's sacred shrines, his spirit has returned to the ocean depths, where he will lead his people for the next one hundred years before returning to earth. Blessed be his name. Burial arrangements will be announced soon. Children of the kingdom, you must begin now to prepare yourself to pay your last respects to Kaabiyesi the Great."

Kaabiyesi dead?!

An announcement from the Kaita Beach Local Government a few hours later declared a two-week period of mourning, during which time the flag was to be flown at half-mast. According to the announcement, the governor had given his approval for the funeral to be held on Christmas Eve at Kaita Beach.

"Since when does the burial of anyone require the approval of a governor?" wondered Prinzi.

"Well, their Kaabiyesi wasn't 'anyone' to them. Besides, what else does Omo-ale do other than connive with the Kaitas of this world?" said Razaki.

"Since Kaabiyesi Island is their Mecca, how come they're not conducting the burial like that of a sheikh?"

"The 'Roko! Perhaps their Kaabiyesi is, or was, everything to them. After all, Haile went to Kaabiyesi Island and came back a *chief*, not an *alhaji*. And don't forget that Kaabiyesi had a number of shrines."

"Did this Kaabiyesi exist at all?"

"If he did not, who then are they going to bury?"

"Oh, that can be arranged," said Efe, who had hurried to the café on hearing the news.

"Are you suggesting they planned the incident?"

"It's not impossible."

"With your power of imagination, you're just wasting

away," Prinzi told her. "So, what happens now?"

"The king is dead. Long live the king. Have you noticed that Kaita has adopted Kaabiyesi's preferred salutation: 'Children of the kingdom'?"

"Again, they've managed to be one jump ahead. Kaabiyesi was supposed to die at the end of this century, not two years before."

"No, I think their day is passing and ours is already dawning."

One week before the funeral, Haile announced a work-free week for all civil servants and created a task force to clean up the environment. Shanka, who postponed the opening of the Kaita Beach Resort indefinitely, made known the burial site – inside the Palace of Good. Tony St Oris returned to Radio Kaabiyesi, where he and Double C ran a twenty-four-hour broadcast of somber music, commentaries on the life and times of Kaabiyesi, and condolence messages from all corners of the globe. Kaita commissioned a marble mausoleum and began to prepare a feast.

Centigrade declared himself a qualified, sympathetic undertaker. Shanka, the head of the funeral committee, declined his services. Ray offered to say ninety-nine special prayers for the dead to ease Kaabiyesi's transition. Shanka turned down the offer. Instead, he engaged Pastor David to hold a daily service of songs to mark Kaabiyesi's passage. The pastor forgot his professed aversion to idols and allowed a stone crocodile to be installed in the church as Kaabiyesi's personal symbol.

And then it began to rain, a persistent clatter that lasted seven days and nights.

"Which one be this one again?" complained Opio.

"How rain go fall non-stop for inside harmattan?"

"They say everything wey dey world dey cry for Kaabiyesi, *abi* you never hear?" said Idi.

"Na so they go talk, but I sure say they don hire serious rainmaker. I don use my own power, plus the one wey Zik of Africa teach me, try to stop am. As I dey see am so, this rain no carry ordinary hand."

"Because the thing no 'gree you stop?" queried Chief Tanker.

"Look you! You know how many times when I make rain or stop am for Uzuakoli? Who you think send water go comot that Kaabiyesi?"

"See your mouth as e be, like Biafra bunker. When Kaabiyesi dey, fear dey 'gree you even look im island?" Idi said.

"No let Kaabiyesi hear you-o. Na travel they say e travel, no be say e die finish. You see this rain? Maybe accident don happen for God laboratory be that. I be Jesse someone, and na we know water reach im hometown."

"My own be say the rain good somehow," said Orita. "How else man for get better umbrella?"

Shanka had distributed jumbo-sized umbrellas bearing Kaabiyesi's personal symbol to all the residents. He apparently wanted nothing to prevent their presence at the funeral.

The day finally arrived, after a wake during which Pastor David broke his previous record for histrionics, Shanka for the importation of bands, Kaita for festivity. The wake witnessed the appearance of nine night masquerades. But there was no corpse, only a luminous stone crocodile.

The corpse arrived from the direction of Kaabiyesi Island in the morning, in a casket that was a miniature replica of the Palace of Good. Kaabiyesi, the word spread, was to be buried sitting. The pallbearers were four crocodile-masquerades. At the fore of the procession were nine clean-shaven, old men, each dressed only in a loincloth and neck beads and carrying either a bowl of fire or of incense. At the rear was a long line of masquerades from all over the country. Hornblowers and drummers accompanied the procession. It was quite a spectacle.

As the procession neared the Palace of Good, human-shaped fire columns appeared, as if from nowhere. Four in all, each appearing from a different direction, they were literally mobile columns of fire – something that no one in Kaita Beach or its environs, including Razaki who was known to be interested in stage effects, had ever beheld.

Then the guests began arriving – a delegation from the federal government, military governors, diplomats, chiefs, and all sorts of men and women in iridescent costumes. The rain continued. Roofs of umbrellas became the skyline of Kaita Beach.

First, the corpse was set in state in the middle of the Palace of Good, causing a surge by people who wanted to see the body of Kaabiyesi. Crowd control measures succeeded in structuring the surge. The figure, which seemed strangely familiar to some of the people, was that of an old man in a damask brocade.

Pastor David said a prayer. Omo-ale, Kaita, and Shanka delivered funeral orations.

Volleys of gunshots, ninety-eight in all, and a feat of hornblowing marked the actual burial. The inscription on the tomb was "Sir El-Kanemi Bello, 1900-1998."

To everyone's amazement, Opio declared that the body in the casket could not be that of "Kaabiyesi." According to him, the body was that of his commander in Biafra. Armed policemen immediately evicted him from the Palace of Good. Outside, he cleared a corner, put a stone at the center and began to march round it, singing the Biafran song for the dead:

> *Enyi-o enyi-o*
> *Enyi-o, enyi-o, enyi*
> *Enyi Biafra alanu-o*
> *Enyi Biafra alaa*
> *Enyi*
> *Enyi Biafra alanu-o*
> *Enyi Biafra alaa*
> *Enyi*
> *Chetakwanu 40, 000*
> *40, 000 bu umu Biafra*
> *Enyi*

Inside, Haile read Kaabiyesi's will. "Children of the kingdom, the day has come at last, and I have gone to lead my other people in their own struggle. It is a struggle that I know very well. The struggle is my life. While I am away, I leave all my rights to Kaita Alhaji Kaita. And to you all, children of the kingdom, I bequeath my cows. Even in my absence, I am with you in spirit. Remain blessed."

And, suddenly, the rain ceased and the sun appeared, coyly at first.

At that point, Ashikodi began to walk on his head, ventriloquially enumerating the names of Kaabiyesi, Omo-ale, Kaita, Shanka, and Haile backward. He then stormed out of the Palace of Good with Segi and Asampete. Razaki, who had brought a video camera to record the event, and Efe – who was covering the funeral for the wire service – stayed on.

Prinzi left One behind and hurried back to his café, where he sat with determination at his desk. Somewhere in the distant background, he heard "Christmas Polka" coming from a radio that had remained tuned to the Christmas Eve. But, more important to him then, the words of his *Invisible Chapters* finally came to him, surging like a storm:

Finally, the sunshine. I can almost smell it. For the past seven days and nights, it had rained fishes and flood in this haven of the poor. Was the rain the laughter of an apocalypse or was it the farewell that nature, even in the harmattan season, bade to 'Kaabiyesi the Great, the Prince of the Atlantic'? There was a storm surge, yes. And there was a funeral. And a corpse. Yet who among us can tell with any certainty whether Kaabiyesi was taciturn fact or brilliant fiction? Was he, indeed, Sir El-Kanemi *Bello or an errand fable masked as reality by land-grabbers and barons? Was he a commander in the Republic of Biafra or a profitable adaptation of the mystique of the Kanem-Bornu Empire inspired by a malleable history of the peoples and empires of West Africa?*

Tonight, the people are marking his stormy passage, his announced return to the depths of the Atlantic, but how many among them are pondering his essence, the meaning of his meaning? I, Prinzi, I shall stay awake, therefore, so that no one shall sleep. *Do I think too highly of myself? Do I believe too faithfully in my possibilities? I have to. I have no other meaning. And I do know that, in the final analysis, reality is only a vision at work, an invisible chapter fulfilled by belief and praxis.*

———

Malaika Palace
Lagos, Nigeria
December 21, 1998

www.ingramcontent.com/pod-product-compliance
Lightning Source LLC
LaVergne TN
LVHW041932070526
838199LV00051BA/2785